MW00639292

DEAD MALL

Part I

Welcome to Halcyon

To Mark,
Thanks for
reading!
S.C.

ALSO BY S.G. TASZ

Veiled Threats

The Long Moon

The Mourning Sun

An Original Sin

The First Shift
(as The First Shift: A Dead Mawl Omnibus)

DEAD MALL

WELCOME TO HALCYON

S.G. Tasz

The Uglycat Press
Las Vegas, NV

Copyright © 2020 by S.G. Tasz

Editing services provided by Chimera Editing
www.chimeraediting.com

Cover art by Joseph Reedy.

ISBN: 978-1-7340752-3-6

To family near and far, far away.

Chapter One

Charlie slid the mop across the cobblestones, keeping his head down to avoid the grimacing eyes of Atlas looming overhead. It had always creeped him out, that tortured look on the planet-saddled Titan's face, as if the sculptor had captured him in the moment before his strength failed. A spigot on top of the globe sent water cascading into the shallow pool below the statue when the place was open. But it was after midnight now and the fountain, like everything else, stood silent and still.

He splashed the mop into the yellow plastic bucket, letting the water dribble off the soaked yarn a little longer than necessary before slopping it onto the floor. The thick silence once again filled the room like a heavy cotton quilt, constricting his chest and sealing his mouth. Taking a single breath felt like a grave offense.

And yet without that stifled nothingness, he wouldn't have heard the soft scuffle behind him, the subtle *chk-chk-chk* near the entrance of Ripped! Fitness and Nutrition.

He wouldn't have made sure to keep his head down and his shoulders loose to project oblivious calm.

He wouldn't have swerved the mop in such a way

that he could pull the six-inch Bowie knife from his belt without breaking his natural movement.

He would not have whipped around to upset the ambush in a perfect fake out.

At least, it would have been perfect—except that there was no one there.

"Hello?" he demanded of the empty hallway, keeping his voice low so as not to ruffle the overly sensitive silence. "Is someone here?"

No answer. No movement. Only the silence, resealing its soft, smothering self around him even thicker than before. He tightened his grip on the knife as his palms started to sweat. He *had* heard something. He was almost certain of it. Then again, dead silence was a tricky thing. You could listen with all your might, and in the end, it would turn out to be nothing. Nothing but your own blood racing through your veins.

Chk-chk-chk.

His ears perked. *That* wasn't nothing. That was the same scuffling sound, behind him again.

No. Not just behind.

You idiot, he thought, rolling his eyes in self-reproach. You know better than that. You know better than to avoid looking up.

Flipping his knife so the blade stood upright, he crouched, then sprang, pivoting in the air as he prepared to attack. Another perfectly executed move, save for one thing: the wet, slippery floor. Instead of whirling into a coordinated strike, his ankle wrenched to the right and sent him sprawling into the fountain. He roared as his head smashed into the strongman's knee and his consciousness wavered into blackness.

Chk-chk-chk.

He hit the water face first, and the sting of chlorine

in his nostrils and eyes yanked him back to reality. Flailing his arms and legs, he finally managed to roll onto his back. He'd made the mistake of averting his gaze once already, and he'd be damned if he let it happen again.

Which meant he had the perfect view when the slumped, salivating thing lurking on top of the world leapt from its perch and dove straight for him. He grunted as it plowed its full weight into his stomach.

And here he'd thought the silence had made it hard to breathe.

The creature grinned at him, its teeth slick with foul, brown saliva. It had him dead to rights, with the emphasis on "dead." He should have been afraid. Instead, searing anger burned hot and powerful through his shaking limbs.

"Go on then," he snarled up at the hideous face. "Kill me. But you better make it fast. My friends are coming. And when they find you, they are going to rip your fucking head off."

The creature only smiled wider. It raised its gnarled hands. Bony fingers curled into claws, each one ending in a sharp, ragged fingernail.

He screamed, a primal, furious noise right into the hideous face. He would not be intimidated. He would not look away.

It plunged its jagged talons into his cheeks. Blood spurted into his eyes. The roar of anger became a shriek of pain.

After that, he saw nothing at all.

Chapter Two

Cari tipped her nose up to the narrow slit at the top of the Prelude's passenger side window. The frosted January air smelled like dust and gasoline as it brushed her cheeks and rustled the knot of hay-colored hair gathered at the base of her neck. Not exactly fresh, but better than the smell of stale cigarettes baked into the car's interior. Bald tires crunched over the frozen dirt road as they sped through the desert. Out the window was sand, a few scraggly creosote bushes—and nothing else. Only this road, the gray line of mountains in the distance, and a landscape so barren it almost made her believe the car was a spaceship, and they were not in Nevada, but on the moon.

"Don't stare like that," Libby grunted from the driver's seat, the slim cigarette bouncing between her lips. "People will think you're on drugs."

Cari snorted at the empty scenery. "What people?"

Her mother's eyes smoldered, but she didn't say anything else. Her caved-in cheeks hollowed even more as she sucked on her cigarette. She was an emaciated woman with hunched shoulders, short wavy hair that was so blond it was almost white, and skin as pale as the winter landscape surrounding them. To the outside world, Libby looked as meek as a nun, and Cari suspected she did everything she could to reinforce that assumption. She wore thick round glasses that took up half her face and bland, shapeless clothes, like today's ankle-length jean dress and white wool sweater, both of which were at least three sizes too big. But Cari knew her mother for real, which meant she was maybe the only person in the world who got to see the person behind the persona.

She snorted again. *Lucky me.*

The dirt road ended in a T-intersection with a paved county highway, where Libby turned right. A mile or so later they passed a pitted green sign. "Welcome to Halcyon. The City of Fortune. Population: 508." Beyond the sign, the empty desert continued, broken only by rotting wooden billboards with faded signs advertising goods and services long gone. Without those, it would be impossible to tell that they had entered a city, let alone what had once been the site of the largest precious metal mine in west-central Nevada.

The road curved to the left, cresting over a hill and diving into a shallow valley. At the bottom, a handful buildings huddled between the left side of the road and the foot of a modest range of red and purple peaks. Buildings littered the slope as well, growing older and more antique the further up one looked, while the structures on the ground were nothing more than dull, gray cubes. Cari noted the familiar storefronts as they trundled by. Bar. Strip club. Another bar. Payday loans. All shuttered and in various states of disrepair. The sight always made her chest ache. Even though she was only sixteen, Cari knew that if places like *that* couldn't suck enough money out of people to make a go of it, things must be worse than bad.

They ran through town in seconds, plunging back into the raw desert as the road morphed from a two-way street into a divided highway. The car's motor coughed and rumbled, struggling to meet the speed demands of its new circumstances. It didn't have to suffer long—the first exit would get them there. Cari could already see the pink and red swirled dome of the Edensgate Shopping Center, shining like an opal on top of the sprawling single-story complex. A little further and she could make out the details of the ecru faux-marble exterior, embellished with Corinthian columns and arches like the Colosseum—or at least like the pictures of the Colosseum she'd seen in her Ancient History textbook. She'd always been fascinated by the design of the mall, mostly because it was so different than anywhere else in town. It was rumored that the architect who'd designed Edensgate had worked on the monolithic Caesar's Palace resort in Las Vegas. Whether that was true or some local BS, the similarities were undeniable. Especially today—the strobing red and blue police lights were as brilliant as any Vegas neon.

"Whoa," Cari said. "That's weird. I wonder—"

Her chest slammed against her seatbelt, knocking the breath out of her lungs as the car screeched to a halt.

"What are you doing?" she wheezed at her mother. "You can't just stop in the middle of the highway!"

Libby ignored her. She sat silent, staring at the police cruiser with perfectly round eyes. Her hands gripped the steering wheel like she was trying to strangle it, and the cigarette trembled in her lips, sprinkling ash all over her lap.

She looks terrified, Cari thought, rubbing the spot on her chest where the seatbelt had assaulted her. But why? It was just a police cruiser. No reason to think the cop would give them a second look.

Unless…

"Mom, have you been drinking again?"

Libby whirled on her daughter, her blue eyes cold and furious. "What did you say to me?"

"Nothing!" Cari shrank back against the door. "I just…you saw the cops and stopped in the middle of the highway and you seem nervous so I was just thinking that maybe one reason would be—"

"Enough!" her mother spat out. "I've had it with your disrespect. You've been acting like a brat all morning, and I'm sick of it." She snatched up the army green backpack at Cari's feet and launched it at her. "Get out of my sight."

Cari gaped at her, clutching her backpack to her chest like a shield. "We're on the highway, Mom. I can't—"

"Out! Get out of my car right *now*!" Libby lunged forward as her left hand pulled back, palm flat and sharp as a blade.

"Okay, I'm going!" Cari fumbled with the handle until it turned, releasing her to onto the thankfully deserted highway. "Sorry."

Libby didn't wait for her to close the door before she hit the gas. Cari jumped back as the car flung itself into the nearest turnaround and fishtailed back down the highway, the door at last swinging closed in response to the vehicle's wide swerves.

"Thanks for the ride," she mumbled at the receding bumper. "Love you too."

She shuffled over to the relative safety of the

shoulder, pulling her sweatshirt more tightly around her as a midwinter gale bit through the thin fabric and burrowed into her skin. It was a quarter mile to the exit lane. She'd have to walk fast if she was going to avoid frostbite. At least there wasn't any snow—her sneakers were way too thin to hold up against any kind of drift.

To avoid thinking about the miserable conditions, she focused on the scene that had just taken place, turning it over in her mind to try to figure out what the hell just happened. Libby had been pretty defensive at the accusation that she'd been drinking again. She also hadn't denied it. But Cari checked all the normal hiding places every day before she went to work and after she got home. If Libby had been ferreting booze, she would have found it.

On the other hand, her mother was at home all day, thanks to her disability pay and what was left of her husband's meager life insurance policy. Who knows what all she got up to?

Or who got up to it with her.

Cari stumbled as she veered onto the exit ramp, the sense of impending doom compounding the lost feeling in her toes.

Nelson.

The name of filled her with anger almost hot enough to thaw her tingling limbs. Yes, it had to be him. Her mother had thought she'd kept it a secret, explaining the left-behind sweaters and sunglasses by saying that, in his capacity as their neighborhood prayer circle leader, he was providing her individual counseling. It sounded plausible, and Cari had wanted to believe it. Had tried desperately to believe it. Then she'd found a used condom wedged between the couch cushions. That discovery had prompted a sixty-minute shower and the certainty that her mother was lying to her.

And if Libby was lying about having the affair, that would cover any party favors her lover happened to bring along on his little visits, wouldn't it?

Her teeth chattered as she finally reached the bottom of the exit ramp. The turn-in for the mall was still several hundred yards away. Rather than prolong her frigid misery, Cari turned off the sidewalk and slid down the shallow embankment into the parking lot. Still cold, but at least she was out of the wind.

Edensgate had four main entrances, each facing a cardinal direction, and each presided over by a carving of the corresponding god in the recessed triangular space above the door. The cruiser idled in front of the east entrance, which featured a winged man sailing above a pasture, vase in hand, pouring water over the fields below. Beneath that, the marble frieze contained a series of deep gashes that looked vaguely like letters, but more like decorative nonsense. And beneath *that* stood a heavy-set officer in the process of ripping down the caution tape that had been strung between the columns on either side of the door. He was middle-aged with a big brown mustache and the lumpy appearance of life-long privilege. His dark eyes tracked her as she approached, narrowing more and more with every step she took. By the time she mounted the sidewalk, he was squinting at her as if he were staring at the sun.

"Help you?" he grumbled.

"Just going to work," she murmured, dropping her eyes submissively. "What happened? Is this a crime scene?"

"Accident. Some janitor fell into the fountain and

cut himself up pretty bad. Made one hell of a mess."

"Oh, no." She peered at the tinted sliding doors but couldn't see anything beyond her own reflection. "That's awful."

"Uh-huh" He tossed the ball of plastic ribbon into a nearby trash can. "Shouldn't you be in school?"

Her jaw tightened. Despite the cold, a bead of sweat formed on her neck. She suppressed the urge to slap it away. "It's, uh, still winter break. School doesn't start up again until *next* week."

"Oh…yeah. I suppose that's right."

He frowned but stepped out of the way to let her through. She could feel him studying her as she passed, his frown deepening, as if he were trying to remember where he had seen her face before. She ducked her head further and kept moving, happy at last when the dark doors cut through the space between them and severed the look.

Technically, she hadn't lied to him. It *was* winter break, and school *was* closed for the rest of the week. Not that it mattered to her, of course.

But he hadn't asked about that, now had he?

Chapter Three

Even though she'd come through the east entrance a thousand times or more, the sight never failed to take her breath away. A lush hand-painted sky covered the ceiling, illuminated by soft white light and trimmed with gold-leafed cornices. Directly overhead, the golden chariot of Helios burst forth, trailing a blaze of orange and yellow sunbeams while a choir of cherubs looked on in awe. As the corridor stretched away, the colors deepened from sunrise to twilight as the fresco cascaded down the opposite wall a hundred yards away, melding with a giant mosaic of sapphire glass studded with shards of twinkling mirror. The corridor itself looked like an ancient city street: storefronts along both sides, with fake windows and balconies affixed to the walls above them and a floor tiled with fashionably uneven cobblestones. It was all so detailed, so lovely—and so very empty.

The mall had been built in the mid-nineties, back when the town still enjoyed unparalleled wealth courtesy of the Halcyon gold mine that had been basically printing money since the 1800s. That all ended eight years ago, when the mine coughed up the last of its shiny rocks and nearly everyone in town was instantly out of a job. The younger, more capable population left town for greener pastures. The rest—whether they were old, sick, or simply in denial that the ride was truly over—survived by any means necessary. Some went on welfare. A few took to the streets. One guy went to Vegas and let a German tourist eat his kidney, or so she'd heard. Either way, nobody needed high-end boutiques or fancy restaurants anymore. There had been one renovation attempt shortly after the mine shut down, probably to try and stem the bleeding with tourism, but it hadn't worked. Now all that remained in the once-grand complex were a few low-rent specialty shops, a shabby second-run movie theater that was only open for two matinees a day (if that), and the Suttermill Department Store, the mall's last anchor tenant. Until three o'clock this afternoon, that is. Then it too would go the way of The Dinosaur—a kitschy archeology-themed gift shop that had somehow held on until just last summer—and Cari's job would go with it.

Inhaling the sweet, semi-perfumed air, Cari made her way toward the arched window opposite the entrance with the words Guest Relations carved into the faux masonry above it. Why a mall as dead as this one needed a greeter, she had no idea. Not that she was complaining. It was nice to see a friendly face first thing in the morning, to have someone smile at her, wave hello, and at least pretend to be happy to see her. Ordinarily he had a wave and hello locked and loaded before she was even through the door.

But not today. Today, he was too busy trying to see around the corner into the main rotunda to register that she had entered the building. A man in his early 60s, with a round face and curly graying hair, he looked like a slightly younger version of Santa Claus.

She paused next to the window out of his sight, trying to see what he was seeing. Even standing practically at his elbow, it still took him a good thirty seconds to sense that he was not alone.

"Oh!" he shouted as he recoiled back into the window. Clutching his chest, he at last offered her an embarrassed smile. "My apologies. I'm afraid I'm a bit…distracted today."

She smiled back. "I get it. Big events going on I hear."

"Uh, yes. Quite." He dropped his eyes to the desk and what looked like a stack of blank papers. "Have a nice day."

"You too." She continued down the hall toward the wide brick archway leading into the rotunda. The area above the arch opened onto the second-floor observation balcony, giving the impression that one was walking under a bridge. On the other side, the marbled glass dome cast a dusty pink light on the piazza below, most of which was occupied by the one-and-a-half story fountain depicting the Greek god Atlas, genuflecting as the world lay heavy upon his shoulder blades. A pair of idle escalators led up to the balcony and the remains of the food court. Another series of storefronts lined the rotunda's perimeter, all caged and blank except for the Black Lotus Defensive Arts Academy, which was only open three days a month, and Ripped! Fitness and Nutrition, open four hours a day and pulling about as many customers.

Cari shivered. As fond as she was of Edensgate, the vibe of the rotunda was undeniably creepy.

The new red tint in the fountain water didn't help

either.

"It was this new mopping solution we're using, sir." The words, spoken in a deep, calm voice, echoed in the all-but-empty space. "It's more concentrated than the old stuff. Charlie probably used too much without thinking, and maybe didn't look where he was walking, and…it was an accident."

Peeking around the fountain, Cari spotted a trio of people. One of them she recognized as Sam, the pudgy, middle-aged assistant manager, clad in his typical drab business shirt and khakis. He stood with his hands on his hips, scowling up at the other two, a man and woman whom Cari did not recognize. The man wore a green button-down shirt and black cargo pants. A green baseball cap covered his short blonde hair. He looked a little like a cop, only instead of a badge, a logo of a padlock with wings graced his left breast pocket. The woman's green coveralls had the same logo in the same place. She was slightly shorter than her counterpart, with russet brown skin and curly black hair tied up in a navy-blue bandanna. She stood with her back half-turned on the men, chewing her thumbnail and staring at the floor, as if waiting for the soonest possible chance to flee

"Don't treat me like an idiot, Cooper," Sam railed. "I know how things are in this town. I know Ray has been letting this place go to hell because that's just what happens around here. But *I'm* not from around here. And I refuse to be sabotaged, not out of resentment and certainly not out of incompetence."

"Yes, Mr. Berger," the guard named Cooper said. "I promise that's not what's happening. Right, Grace?"

The woman shrugged but didn't look up.

"Anyway," he continued, "We've contacted the

fountain maintenance company in Carson City, and they said they can be out here to flush the system in a few days."

"*Days?*" Sam screeched. "I've got site visits scheduled. I don't think the Wal-Mart executives are going to react well to a blood fountain."

"You sure about that?" Grace muttered under her breath.

Sam turned on her. "What did you say? Because unless it was some brilliant insight about how to fix this—"

"With all due respect," Grace said, in a tone that contained none, "making you look good for a bunch of...*investors*, is not my job."

He glowered at her. "It is if I say it is."

"We don't work for you."

"But your firm does. What do you suppose your boss will say when I tell him his shift managers aren't acting like team players?"

Her brown eyes flashed with sudden fury. "What do *you* know about being part of a team?"

"Grace—" Cooper began.

"Now you listen to me, little man." She towered over Sam, who did his best not to cower. "What happened to Charlie is horrifying. I'm sick over it. And now you have the nerve to question *my* loyalty? What the hell gives you the right?"

"Okay, okay." Sam held up his hands. "I didn't know you took waste removal so seriously."

She seemed about to say something else when Cooper dropped a hand on her shoulder. She blinked at the touch, as if waking up from a trance. After a moment, she allowed him to pull her back in line.

Cari frowned. Something about the way he was

looking at Grace seemed…odd. Given the outburst, she would have expected him to be angry or embarrassed. Instead, he looked nervous, like an older sibling who knew they were on the verge of getting away with something but hadn't quite managed it yet. Be cool, it said. A few more minutes and we'll have done it. Just. Be. Cool.

"Okay, fine," Sam huffed, running a hand through his hair. "So we have a blood fountain for a few days. How can we work with that? Let's brainstorm. Um…we could get some pumpkins and a few of those fake spider webs and arrange them all around the fountain. Tell them we're preparing for a Halloween in spring promotion." He shook his head in disgust. "No, no. That's a terrible idea. Haunted crap only sells in October."

"Yeah," Grace said as Cari shuffled covertly past them. "*That's* why it's a terrible idea."

The metal security gates were still shut when Cari arrived at Suttermill. She would have opened them, but they were so old and stiff in their tracks that it was impossible for one person to slide them more than a few inches without help. As she pried the gates apart wide enough for her to squeeze through, she wondered why anyone still bothered closing them at all. Suttermill had been slowly selling off its inventory for three months. Now, on its last day of existence, there was almost nothing left except for the display tables, mannequins, and a few items too ugly to sell.

Her sneakers squeaked on the linoleum as she walked down the center aisle past the darkened makeup counter, its brilliant white bulbs having cast the last of their judgments on the women of Halcyon long ago.

On the other side of the aisle was an army of holiday decorations. Tinsel reindeer, garlanded trees and red ball towers clustered in what had once been the shoe section. At the far end, a rosy-cheeked elf statuette offered up a perfectly wrapped present to passers-by, a sign propped against its feet: "Free If You Can Ho Ho Haul 'Em Away." She bopped the fluffy green and white striped bow as a hollow sadness panged her chest.

Cari had only been working at Suttermill since last June, but nonetheless she had come to think of it as home. Better than home. It was a haven, a place where she could feel halfway normal for a few hours. That had been especially vital since September, when her mother had refused to let her set foot in "that bastion of corruption and immorality," aka Halcyon High School. At first, Cari had dismissed it as another one of her mother's fickle crusades, taken up in a passion and dropped almost as quickly. Instead, it proved to be the one mission Libby decided to see all the way through. She filed the paperwork and made her case to the school board, all the while giving a tour de force performance of a loving, caring mother. And of course, they believed her. Why wouldn't they? She was the picture of parental concern. After that iron curtain had fallen, the Suttermill job had been Cari's only reprieve.

And now it was ending. The trucks were coming later today to pack up everything that hadn't sold. The hideous tablecloths. The chipped coffee cups. The reindeer and the elf. All would go, and it would be over.

What the hell was she going to do tomorrow, when all she had was her mother?

And...Nelson?

She jerked herself away from the thought. Today

was still today, and she would enjoy it as best she could, for as long as she could. All. Day. Long.

"You're late," Holly grumbled as Cari arrived at the register, her eyes never leaving her clipboard.

"Sorry. My mom dropped me off at the wrong door," Cari said, hoping her breezy tone would disguise the lie. "How are you?"

"Shitty," Holly snapped. "I had to pull an all-nighter moving stuff onto the loading dock. I only got about twenty minutes of sleep, and that was because I literally passed out at my desk."

Cari shoved her backpack and sweatshirt into a cubby under the counter, taking a surreptitious look around the store as she did so. For having worked all night, Holly had left a lot of stuff on the floor. In fact, the only thing that backed up Holly's story was Holly herself. Frosty blue eyeshadow caked her sunken eyes and her wavy blond hair was greasy and mussed. She even wore the same low-cut, shimmery magenta blouse from the day before, though based on the obvious seams and exposed tag, it appeared to be inside out. Not that Cari was going to tell her—she was in a bad enough mood already.

"If you needed help, you could have called me," Cari said, pinning her name tag to her buttoned-up blue shirt. "I wouldn't have minded."

Holly chuckled bitterly and rolled her eyes. "Why? So the district manager could rip my head off for making a sixteen-year-old load trucks in the middle of the night? You'd love that, wouldn't you?"

Instead of defending herself, Cari stayed silent. This happened sometimes with Holly. She would make weirdly paranoid accusations that seemed to come out of nowhere and would disappear just as quickly. Best thing to do was just be quiet—and then change the subject.

"So…were you here when that janitor guy fell?"

"No," Holly said around a yawn. "I was probably in the truck bay when it happened."

Cari frowned. "But I heard he was seriously injured. You didn't hear him splashing or screaming, or—"

"I said I didn't see anything, okay?" Holly snapped. "I only found out an hour ago when Sam told me about it."

"Okay. Sorry," Cari said, allowing the outburst to roll off her back once again. In the relatively short time Cari had known her, Holly had never been a particularly sunny person. But that hadn't always been the case. Apparently, she'd been life of the party in high school, at least the way Holly told it. And smart too—she'd been on her way to Stanford when the mine crapped out and the money dried up. Now here she was, stuck in a town with no prospects and no way out. Sure, she was still a monster bitch. But at least Cari could understand why.

"What is going on with Sam anyway?" Cari pressed the no sale button and the register dinged open. She began counting down the register. "Seems weird that an assistant manager would come all the way from San Francisco when Ray lives a mile down the road."

"Ray's out," Holly said around a yawn. "Heart disease. From what I heard, the corporate owners were thinking about cutting their losses and selling the place when Sam stepped in. I don't know what he said to them, but it must have been pretty convincing because they promoted him on the spot. I guess he thinks he can resurrect this dump somehow." She glared at Cari. "If any new jobs come up for grabs, I call dibs. Got it?"

Cari nodded stiffly. Satisfied, Holly turned her attention back to her clipboard. That's the way it was with adults in this town ever since the mine closed. Looking out for number one came before everything else. Even kids. *Especially* kids. For whatever reason, anyone in their mid-twenties and beyond seemed to have a special iron maiden in their hearts for the children of Halcyon.

Cari slammed the register closed and checked her watch. Eight AM. "Time to open," she muttered in Holly's direction.

"Mm-hmm," Holly murmured dreamily.

Something in Holly's tone sent a shiver up her neck. Despite having acknowledged the statement, Holly still stood with her back to Cari and her head bent down, rigid except for her hand, which jerked and spasmed as it dragged the pen across the clipboard. When Cari peered at what she was writing, the shiver increased. Instead of words or numbers, the page was covered with angular, nonsensical scrawls.

"Holly?" Cari ventured her hand forward to tap Holly on the shoulder.

Holly whipped around, emitting a wheezy gasp. It was as if she had forgotten Cari was there.

"What?" she practically screamed.

For a moment, Cari couldn't answer. She was too distracted by Holly's eyes. The right one was its normal brilliant green, but the other was as dark as coal. And not just the iris either.

Holly's entire left eye had gone completely black.

"*What*, Cari?"

Cari blinked. Holly stood with her hands on her hips, staring at her impatiently with two perfectly normal eyes.

"Uh, I'm s-sorry," Cari spluttered. "It's…it's eight o'clock and the doors are still mostly shut, so…"

Holly gazed toward the front of the store, then back at Cari. "Oh. Okay." The half-irritated, half-exhausted tone in her voice was the closest Holly ever came to an apology.

Cari stepped aside to let Holly out from the behind the counter. She watched with a furrowed brow as Holly struggled to pull back the sticky gates. It must have been a trick of the light. Or maybe exhaustion. Maybe she was overtired, and she had seen something that wasn't there. Either way, there was nothing wrong with Holly now.

"Cari! Get your skinny behind up here and help me!"

At least, nothing more than usual.

Chapter Four

It was a long slog until lunchtime. Everything worth buying had been snatched up weeks ago, and the store was open several hours before they had their first customer. Then things picked up. *Way* up. The news of the tragic accident at the Atlas fountain had hit the town and everyone wanted to be the first to see where it happened. Once they'd finished gawking and taking pictures, they were left with the question of what to do next. They had driven all the way out here, after all, and Suttermill *was* closing today. It got so busy that, for the first time in weeks, Holly had to jump on a second register to keep the lines moving. By the time things slowed down, it was half past one.

"Take your lunch," Holly said, bracing herself against the counter with one hand and wiping her forehead with the back of the other. Her sallow cheeks had grown greenish, the dark circles around her bloodshot eyes now a deep midnight purple.

"Are you sure?" Cari asked. It wasn't like Holly to let her take lunch first. "I mean, no offense, but you don't look so good."

"I'm fine!" Holly snapped. "Go."

Cari ducked her head in apology. Operating on no sleep wasn't doing anything to improve Holly's innate surliness, which made Cari even less inclined than usual to contradict her. She grabbed her bag from under the counter and went in search of sustenance.

As she left Suttermill, her eyes meandered across the rotunda to the stilled fountain. An eerie feeling wriggled up her neck as she stared in horrified fascination at the brilliant red puddle lapping at Atlas's feet and the white marble globe stained with rust-colored streaks.

It looked like the world had bled to death.

She tore herself away from the ghoulish scene and darted into the Edensgate Cinema before it could draw her back in. As soon as the smell of burnt popcorn hit her, the eerie feeling dissipated. The small lobby enveloped her, with its dingy purple carpet and overheard lights that always had at least four on the fritz. It didn't look like much, but it was the only place in the mall where she could find something that resembled lunch.

To the uninitiated, the food court would seem a more logical choice, but it was a long walk for a short drink—the vending machines were half-stocked on a good day, and the food always seemed to be on the verge of expiration. As strange as it was, the theater was the safer option.

She bypassed the empty ticket booth and headed straight for the concessions counter. A black-clad figure lay sprawled face down across the glass with his head wrapped in his arms. She grinned at her good fortune. Padding silently across the carpet to stand in front of him, Cari raised her hands high, then slammed them down on the counter near his ears.

He shot upright with such force that he nearly toppled backward into the soda machine. The thick loop of chain connecting his belt to his wallet clattered against the rungs of his stool.

"I wasn't sleeping!" His dark eyes darted back and forth before they landed on her. "Jesus...don't you know you're not supposed to wake a sleeping man? I could have killed you."

She smirked. "Pretty sure the rule is 'Don't wake a sleep*walking* man'. If everyone got murdery because they were awoken unexpectedly, there would be a lot more stabbed alarm clocks."

"I've stabbed, like, a thousand alarm clocks, so..." He yawned and ran a hand through his wavy black hair. "How's it going, Mayhem?"

Cari groaned as she rounded the far end of the counter. "I hate it when you call me that."

His face wrinkled in a hurt-puppy pout. "Why you gotta be so mean to me? It's not my fault that's your name."

"How do you figure that?"

He waggled his eyebrows. "A magician never tells."

"Fine, be that way." She scooped tortilla chips into a partitioned plastic bowl and shellacked them with bright orange goo from the cheese dispenser. "But if you're going to use my dumb nickname, I'm going to use yours, *Rex*."

"If by dumb you mean awesome, then go right ahead."

Cari's exasperated sigh hid her secret relief. At least something about this day felt normal, even if it was simply that Drexel (aka Rex) Ranganathan was still an irritating teenaged boy.

"How's your mom?" Rex asked as she joined him at

the counter.

"Don't ask," she said with a snort. "How's this month's family?"

"*Seriously* don't ask." He swiped a chip from her tray. "Seven kids in a two-bedroom house. I had to shove an air mattress into the crawlspace over the garage. I give it a month. Two, tops."

She shook her head in sympathy. Rex had been meandering through the Halcyon foster system since the sixth grade, when he was the new kid at Trilby Middle School. But his orphan adventures started long before that. He had told her everything about his foster families, about his past lives in Reno and Tahoe and even Vegas for a little bit. Different details, but all with the same "return to sender" finish. Behavioral issues, they said, though Cari suspected it had more to do with the color of his skin, his flashy rebellious streak, and the fact that, with a few regional exceptions, Nevada was a fairly homogenous state. No one wanted their neighbors to accuse them of "raising a terrorist."

"I 'spose you heard about the thing that happened last night? The guy and the fountain?" Rex stabbed at the rapidly congealing cheese with a sharp corner of his chip.

Cari nodded, nibbling the edge of her own. "I heard it was an accident."

"That's what they want you to think," he said. "But do the math. Suttermill is going under, morale is low, no one cares what happens to the stock. Thieves probably figure it's an easy target."

"You think it was a robbery gone bad?"

"Maybe. All I'm saying is that I'm glad our last movie starts at four instead of ten, or I'd be sweeping the floor with one hand and carrying a Molotov cocktail in the other. With an *Anarchist's Cookbook* in my pocket, too. Just in case."

He went in for another chip. Cari swatted his hand away. "You do that now. With the Cookbook I mean, not the Molotov cocktail. I hope."

"You can never be too careful." Rex grinned. "Speaking of tactical combat…"

He stooped and rummaged through a low shelf. When he straightened, he held a slim blue clamshell case featuring a muscle-bound figure in full combat gear, sword in one hand and a gaping, disfigured human head in the other.

Cari squealed, her lunch forgotten. "You got *Splatterfield Three*? I thought it didn't come out until next week."

"It doesn't." He winked at her. "But I know a guy."

She smiled indulgently. As a dedicated member of every video game rewards program he could join for free, it was much more likely that he'd been on some high priority wait list. But she would ignore the fib if it meant she could play the latest installment of the best 1-v-1 brawler *ever* before it hit the shelves.

Rex fired up the game console he kept hidden under the counter (the only good birthday present he'd ever gotten from any of his foster dads) while she mashed buttons on the remote for the wall-mounted television channel. A few clicks later, and the showtime display disappeared. The screen lit up with a blood-soaked meadow where a phalanx of cyborgesque commandos squared off against a rush of zombie-like monsters.

"Best of three?" Rex handed her a wireless controller.

"You're going down." She pressed the Start button.

"Ready?"

"Ready and waiting."

The screen faded up on a craggy gray field with a jagged ravine running down the middle. Three bridges connected the two sides, one of which was in extreme disrepair. On one side, three military units gathered on yellow grass while a massive horde of gray-skinned undead trudged aimlessly in the muddy swamp on the other side. Since they both preferred the precision of the military over the horde's brute strength in the earlier versions, they let the game randomly determine sides. Cari drew the military first. She arranged her units evenly across the battle lanes with a smug smile. Rex, on the other hand, clumped his team in the bottom lane. Maybe it was out of spite at having the less desirable team, or maybe it was because he thought the overwhelming numbers would work to his advantage. But all it did was give her a larger target to aim at. By the time the five-minute timer ran down, the score was an embarrassing 57 to 18.

"Dammit!" Rex exclaimed as a knockoff version of the Star-Spangled Banner trumpeted from the screen's tinny speakers. "I don't know how you do those combos. Are you four-jointed or something?"

"It's quadruple-jointed," Cari said. "And no. I'm just that good."

She reached over to ruffle his hair, but he ducked out of her reach.

"Round Two," he growled. "This time, *I* get the military."

She shrugged. "Loser's option."

He scowled, and they started again. The military side gained an early lead as Rex battered her front line before he regrouped in the middle lane for a late surge.

Cari pretended to grimace while her heart pounded exuberantly. As his team advanced, she moved one of her lurching monsters to stand in front of a breaching Humvee. A jerk of her thumb, followed by three quick taps of her index finger, and the monster grabbed the oncoming vehicle by the passenger door.

"What the—?" Rex's jaw dropped as the screen cut to a closeup of the creature flinging the car back toward the military side of the field. It hit the ground, flipped end over end three times, and took out a third of his team.

"Strike!" Cari yelled over the whooping siren that accompanied her sky-rocketing point total.

"What the hell was that?" Rex demanded, his thumbs mashing furiously at the buttons.

"Battle Bowling," she said. "It was a hidden feature in SF2. I looked it up in the library computer lab last week."

"Does your mom know about that?"

"Does *your* mom know about *this*?" Cari repeated the move, obliterating all but one tank and a handful of his soldiers.

"Son of a bitch!"

Her triumphant laughter was cut short by the sound of the door opening behind her. She turned in her seat as the mall greeter entered the lobby. "Oh…hi."

"Uh, hello," he said, his eyes transfixed by the morbid display on the TV screen. "I'm so sorry to interrupt—"

"Goddammit!" Rex yelled over an explosion followed by a chorus of high-pitched screams. "The military can't throw its own tank? Screw that shit."

"Drexel." Cari elbowed him in the ribs until he turned around.

"Oh! Uh, one sec." Rex fumbled with his controller. The screen froze on a close-up of a zombie's face, its mouth peeled back in a victorious sneer. "Can I help you?"

The greeter cleared his throat. "Actually, I was looking for Ms. Hembert. I didn't mean to disturb you, but I know the store is closing for good soon and there are a few things I'd like to purchase, if I may."

Cari frowned. "Is Holly not there?"

"No. At least, I didn't see anyone."

Her frown deepened. Whatever else Holly may be (and she was a *lot* of things), she took her job seriously. She wouldn't just walk off it without a good reason.

Then again, the store was basically closed. If there was ever a time for *carpe diem*-ing, this was it.

"Okay, then," she sighed. "I guess I'll be right over."

"Great. Thank you." With a smile in Rex's direction, he ambled out.

She handed Rex her controller. "Looks like I'm gonna need a rain check on that tiebreaker."

"Any time, any place." Rex dumped the controllers on the counter. "You want company? It's even deader around here than usual, and I'm due for a break."

She smiled. "A break from napping and getting your ass kicked, you mean?"

"It's harder than it looks." He flipped the TV back to showtimes. "I'll clean up here and be over in a few."

"Sounds good." She slid off her stool. Maybe it wasn't the most responsible thing in the world to bring a friend to work, but Suttermill was in its final hours. What were they gonna do—fire her?

Chapter Five

The greeter waited at the register, a neat pile of ties and sweater vests stacked on the counter in front of him.

"Thank you for cutting your break short," he said as she ran the scan gun over the tags. "I do appreciate it."

Her hand trembled, making it difficult to refold the sweater vest in her hand. She wasn't really sure how to respond to someone saying they appreciated her. For better or worse, it almost never came up.

"Is this really free?"

"Hm?" She glanced up. He was pointing at the present-offering elf. "Oh...yes. It's free. Everything in that section is free. The trees, the reindeer...and I think there's even a Santa costume in the back."

"Just this will do," he said, hooking an arm around the elf's slim waist.

"Of course," she said, stifling a giggle. With the elf in his arm he looked more like Santa than usual, even without the suit.

She swiped his card and handed it back to him. The machines had never been speedy, and today they were slower than ever. She drummed her fingers on the counter. Maybe the Internet had decided to pull a Holly and duck out early. At last, it uttered a surly beep and spit out a curl of paper, which he signed.

"You're all set," she said as she handed him his bag. "Thanks for shopping Suttermill—what's left of it, anyway."

"Of course." He looped his elf-free hand through the plastic handle. "And thank you for your help, Ms. Hembert."

She pointed at her name tag. "Cari."

"Right, Cari." Sans name tag, he simply pointed at his chest. "John."

"John," she repeated. Her polite smile faded moment he turned his back. She had wanted to say, "nice to meet you," but what was the point? She was probably never going to see him again.

A sudden vibration in her pocket demanded her attention. She flipped open her phone to check the caller ID.

Home.

"Shit," she whispered as her stomach started to churn. Her mother never called her at work. She barely called at all—and when she did, it was only because she wanted something.

Bzz.

She could just not answer. After all, she was on the clock. It would be perfectly reasonable if she didn't answer.

Bzz.

But that would only be a stopgap, wouldn't it? A brief delay before the next call. And the next. And the next.

Bzz.

With a sigh, Cari pressed the green button.

"Yes, Mother?"

"Cari dear! Could you pick me up a carton of Menthol Blues before you come home? I'm down to my last pack. I'll pay you back for it, obviously."

Over-enunciated consonants, t's and s's hit so hard they sounded like an aluminum bat against a pipe. Almost enough to hide the slur in her voice.

Almost.

"Fine." Cari gritted her teeth. A dumb question, one she shouldn't ask, escaped her lips. "Anything else?"

"Well, if you're offering…"

There it was. That oh-so-casual tone Cari had heard so many times before. She screwed her eyes closed.

"Can you grab me a six pack too? Nelson came over to help me recover from that little incident we had when I dropped you off at work this morning. You know how good he is when I'm in spiritual distress."

"Oh, I know," Cari said bitterly. *And I bet he brought his friend, Mr. Cuervo. Patron Saint of Distressed Spirits.*

Because he's good like that.

"Yes. And I want to be a good hostess in return. But as you know, I have nothing here to offer him."

Cari's cheeks burned as a low, painful thumping filled her ears. "So, it's true. You *are* drinking again."

Her mother spat out a bitter chuckle. *"Yes, Cari. Now I am."*

Cari sucked air through her nose as full weight of the moment slammed into her gut. Had she been wrong? Had Libby been sober this morning after all? Had her accusation hurt her mother so much it had jostled her right off the wagon?

Was this, in fact, *all her fault?*

On the line came a soft shuffling sound, followed by a hoarse voice. *"Forget it, baby. Hang up and get back over here."*

Cari gripped the phone so tightly the slim edges dug into her hand. Her mother continued talking, but she couldn't hear her—the thumping in her ears had turned into an assault of cannon fire.

Was it her imagination, or had the lights in the store gotten way brighter all of a sudden?

And her clothes...they'd fit this morning, but suddenly they felt two sizes too small.

She flicked her gaze toward the clock on the register—and nearly gasped. How was it almost three already? Her shift was nearly over, and her job at Suttermill was about to disappear.

After that...*this*. And only this. Forever.

"Mayhem?"

She blinked. Across the counter, dark eyes stared at her with intense concern. How long had Rex been standing there?

"Thank you so much, dear." Her mother's cloying voice grated against her eardrum. *"Oh, and one more thing: I'm probably not going to be able to pick you up tonight. I mean, I probably could, but we both know how you feel about that. You can get yourself home, right?"*

"Yeah, sure. Gotta go." Cari managed to slap her phone shut before she sank to the floor.

"Whoa, hey!" Rex's voice tumbled down from above as he vaulted over the counter and knelt at her side. "What's going on?"

"My mom, she...she..."

She...what? She can't pick me up? She's drinking again? Probably because of me?

She hugged her legs and buried her face in her

knees.

"It's okay," Rex soothed, and Cari felt a whisper-soft touch graze her arm. "Just breathe. In and out, okay? In…and out."

He demonstrated. She did her best to follow. Her heart pummeled her lungs like a prizefighter, making it difficult to breathe at all, let alone deep and slow. Concentrating, she forced her lungs to inflate. They ached in protest. She let them relax, then pulled in another full breath, and another, until at last she could feel her muscles start to untwist and her heart return to its normal, non-pugilistic pace. She slumped back against the shelves, her head rolling sideways until it came to rest on Rex's shoulder.

"I don't know why you take her calls," he whispered, his hand still on her arm. "It just messes you up."

Cari shrugged and turned her head her further into him. His t-shirt smelled like popcorn and vaguely ocean-smelling deodorant. "She's my mom."

"I guess." He knocked his forehead lightly against hers. "You want to lay down in the back?"

"I can't," Cari whimpered as she dragged her head up. The wet splotch on Rex's shoulder surprised her. She hadn't even realized she'd been crying. "The movers will be here at three and I think Holly went home sick without telling me and—"

"Don't worry about it," Rex said as he stood up. "I worked closing day at the GameStop, remember? I think I can handle a few ugly sweaters."

She took the hands he offered and pulled herself up. "What about the movie theater?"

Rex shrugged. "The last movie doesn't start until four, and it's some Disney knock-off that's been out since Thanksgiving. No one's into it. I can pull double duty for a few hours."

"But why—"

"No, no. No more questions." He pushed her gently toward the back of the store. "I'll come get you if I run into trouble. Which I won't. Because I'm the best."

She rolled her eyes. "Fine, I'll go. But you'll come get me in an hour, right? I...need to catch the bus before it gets dark."

"Aye aye, Cap'n." Rex saluted.

"Dork." She turned away before he had the chance to see the full extent of her gratitude.

The manager's office contained a cluttered desk, an equally cluttered bulletin board, and a row of lockers where the once-numerous staff members had stored their personal items. A single frosted glass window provided enough light for Cari to see without turning on the fluorescents. Grabbing a tattered Yellow Pages, she slid the chair aside and ducked down into the desk's leg cavity. Heat wafted from the floor-level vent, making the small space much warmer than the rest of the room. Curling into a ball, she wedged the soft, fat book under her head. As the smell of ink and paper filled her nose, she allowed her eyes to roam around the sepia-tinted semi-darkness in the hope that they would eventually tire themselves out. Filing cabinet. The bottom row of lockers. Knockoff Chanel purse. Garbage can.

She yawned. It was working. Chair leg. Another chair leg. Back to the lockers again, and the purse, and the garbage can...

The purse...?

She drifted off before she could finish marveling.

Holly must have been pretty sick to forget her purse at a store that, by tomorrow morning, would no longer exist.

Chapter Six

She swiped an item over the counter-mounted scanner. *Blip.* The line stretched away from her register, further and further, until it practically disappeared into the shadows in the back of the store. A row of people with their arms full of God knows what, shuffling forward only if and when she allowed them to. *Blip.* Another item. *Blip.* Another; something light and innocuous that slipped through her hands without leaving any impression at all. *Blip. Blip. Blip.*

"Have a nice day." She placed the plastic bag on the end of the counter. "Next."

The line shuffled out from the ether. She looked up at her customer.

He didn't have a face. None of them did. They wore normal clothes, had normal hair, stood like normal people, except that where their faces should be was nothing except static, gray and bubbling like an offline television.

The thing in front of her dumped its stack of items on the table. They looked like giant gray Legos, each one with a huge barcode stamped on one side. Her hands worked by themselves, scanning them through.

Blip. Blip. Blip. Her hands gave him his receipt.

"Have a nice day."

He took his bags, turned, and dropped into a deep, dark chasm in the floor.

"Next."

"*Morning!*"

Cari's eyes snapped open. She wasn't at her register. She wasn't even standing up. She was still curled under the desk in the back office.

A dream. Silly her. Of course, it was a dream. They didn't even have a counter-mounted scanner at the front register. Only the guns.

She pressed herself upright, squinting at Rex through the bright office lights. "What time is it?"

"Closing time. You don't have to go home, but...well, you're a minor, so you probably do have to go home."

Cari scooted out from under the desk. Her legs were stiff, and the right side of her face was numb from being pressed against the phone book for so long. Good thing it hadn't been open or she'd probably have the number for Chin's China Garden stamped on her cheek. "You let me sleep all afternoon?"

"What 'let'? You were *out*. I tried to wake you and got *nothing*. I would have thought you were dead if it weren't for the snoring."

She scowled at him. "I do *not* snore."

Rex winked. "Sure, you don't."

"Whatever." Rubbing her eyes, Cari checked her watch. Suddenly she was wide awake. "Shit! It's five to midnight?"

"Yeah, exactly. So, we should probably—"

But Cari was already out the door, wincing at the pins and needles in her shins.

"Hey!" Rex cried. As she dove behind the register to grab her sweatshirt and bag, she could hear him trying to catch up. The clop of his boots and the rattle of his wallet chain were nothing compared to his breathless wheezing. When he finally reached her, his cheeks were flushed and shiny with sweat.

"Thank God that's over."

"Sorry," she said, and took off running again.

"Wait! Don't you need to lock the gate?"

"Leave it! There's nothing left anyway." Of course, that wasn't technically true—a shelf of junk lingered in the back, presumably because it couldn't fit on the trucks, and an army of mannequins stood at attention in the front window. But given the alternative, she was willing to risk a few swiped dish towels.

"Christ, May, what's the rush?" Rex groaned as they blew passed the sanguine Atlas fountain. "The doors are *already* locked. They have been since ten."

"The *primary* locks have been engaged since ten." She wrestled the straps of her backpack over her shoulder. "Those are one-way locks. They still open from this side. But there's a secondary lock that engages at midnight after *everyone* is out. Once it goes on, no one gets through it until six am. In *or* out."

"That's weird," Rex panted. "Still, there's gotta be a back entrance, or an emergency release in case there's a fire or something, right?"

"I don't know," she panted. *And I don't feel like finding out.*

She banked around the corner and passed the empty greeter's window. About ten more feet and she would overtake the east entrance. Six feet. Two. One—

A carton of Menthol Blues.

She stopped dead. Sensing her presence, the

47

automatic door slid open. A tantalizing wisp of icy air brushed against her forehead before the door sealed itself once again. She glanced up at the digital clock above the door that dictated the mall's one true time.

23:57.

She rolled her shoulders, hoping she would feel the stiff corner of a cigarette carton dig into her back. But the bag was too light, too floppy. Too empty.

The doors slid open again, enticing her to accept her failure—and the inevitable punishment that would follow.

Rex shambled to a stop next to her and doubled over, one hand braced against his knee while the other grasped the waistband of his chain-laden jeans to keep them from falling down. "Thank...you," he wheezed. "Almost...died. Now let's...go wait...for the bus...the sweet, sweet bus...with chairs and...sitting..."

Cari took a step backward. The doors closed again. This time, they didn't reopen.

"We can't leave yet."

His face crumbled, and he folded even further over his knees. "Mayhem, you know how much I hate exercise. Can't we—?"

Cari ignored him, sprinting back down the East Hall, past the greeter's window and the the arched bridge, on and on until she reached The Buck Stop Convenience Store. The manager, having made peace with the dimness of the store's prospects long ago, had stopped locking the security gate in the hopes of a major robbery and a big insurance payout (or so Rex had once speculated). Unfortunately for Mr. Manager, almost everything in the place was too crappy to steal, thanks to its random and ever-changing inventory. It was the kind of place where you'd be more likely to find a stuffed squirrel and bag of kazoos than milk, bread and toothpaste. Luckily, booze and cigarettes were two things it always seemed to have in stock.

"Grab a sixer of Red Crown!" Cari shouted behind her as she wheeled around the counter toward the cigarette display.

"Seriously?" Rex panted. "Why do you want to drink that swill?"

"It's not for me." Despite the time crunch, Cari found she had a spare moment to shoot him a "I don't want to talk about this" look.

He nodded, indicating message received, and trotted away.

Cari returned her attention to the shelves behind the counter. They'd reorganized since the last time she'd been on this kind of errand, and the cartons were now on the second-highest one.

"They only have 12 and 24!" Rex shouted from across the store. "Unless you want bottles!"

"Fine!" Cari said. She stretched herself to her full length but couldn't quite reach. Jumping only served to knock them further back. "A little help please!"

Rex materialized next to her so quickly it was almost like magic. "Stand aside, little lady. I'll handle this."

He plucked a carton from the shelf without so much as standing on his toes. Grinning, he tossed it at her. "What would you do without me?"

"I shudder to think," Cari said as she stuffed the box into her bag and tossed a crumpled pair of twenties on the counter, with a mental wave goodbye. Yes, her mother had promised repayment—which meant it was as good as gone.

A siren blasted through the air, smashing the closed

quiet to pieces. She'd heard that alarm before, on the many, *many* nights she'd loitered around the mall until the latest possible moment. It was the all-out warning. In 30 seconds, every door in the building would be locked and sealed until morning.

But back then, she'd already been on the outside, at the bus stop, waiting for the final run of the night. Now…

She looked at Rex. He looked back at her with mounting dread. "Don't say it."

"Run!"

They raced up the East Hall, Rex falling further and further behind her thanks to his sagging pants and complete lack of athletic ability.

That's okay, Cari told herself. I just need to trip the sensor. Prop the door open, buy some more time. Only ten more feet.

Six.

Two.

One.

The siren cut out. In the lingering echo, she lifted her eyes to the clock above the door.

00:00.

Too late.

She raised her hands as she barreled full speed into the glass. The impact made her wrists spark with pain as they jammed back in her sockets. The doors, on the other hand, barely shuddered in their tracks.

"Dammit!" She slapped the door a few times, prompting another flash of pain down her arms. No response. Exhausted, she leaned back against the glass to catch her breath.

"Ugghhhhh." Rex lay sprawled on his back across

the cobblestones, arms outstretched as he gulped greedily at the air. His eyes drooped closed and his cheeks glistened with sweat.

Cari narrowed her eyes. "You saw the clock, didn't you?"

He nodded. "What can I say? I wasn't running that fast."

"And you didn't think to tell *me* before I smashed into the door?"

"I'm sorry! My brain isn't getting enough oxygen. All I knew was that I could *finally* stop."

"Yeah, well, thank God you're such a lightweight. If you were in any better shape you would have slammed into the door. And me. With a six-pack of beer in your arms."

"Glad I could help." He peeled himself off the ground and joined her at the door, the six-pack dangling heavily in his grip. "Your mom's gonna kill you, isn't she?"

"Nah. She probably hasn't even noticed I'm gone," she said. And it was true. Given her mother's likely state of mind at this late hour, she probably wouldn't notice her daughter had yet to come home. But she *would* take offense to the missing beer and cigarettes. For that heinous transgression, the punishment was sure to be severe. And from how Rex was staring at the ground, he knew that as well as Cari did.

"Anyway." Rex ran his free hand through his hair. "You're sure there's no way out?"

She scanned the walls around the door. No buttons, no switches. Nothing that even resembled an emergency release. "If there is, I don't know about it."

"Ah." Rex stood silent for a moment, possibly deep in thought. "Well then…if we're stuck here anyway, how about a movie night? I happen to know there are a couple of those old Universal monster movies in the projection room crawl space. *Dracula, Wolfman,* and I think *Frankenstein* might be up there too. I'll make popcorn, we can scare up some blankets from that tomb of a store you got over there, and we'll have a marathon." He hefted the beer. "We can even toast to your last day."

Cari smiled wistfully. In the chaos of their attempted escape, she'd nearly forgotten that this was her last day. Suddenly, being stuck in the mall on this particular night didn't seem like such a bad thing. "Okay. I'm in."

"Alrighty then, you juvenile delinquent. Let's go!" He swung an arm around her neck in a loose headlock and half-dragged, half-shepherded her toward the rotunda.

"I am *not* a delinquent!" Cari squealed, delivering a light uppercut to his ribs.

"Stealing beer and cigarettes, Ms. Hembert? Oh, it'll be hard time for you, mark my words."

"Others will follow! My revolution will live on! Beer and cigarettes forever!"

"Tell it to the judge."

"I will." She wriggled out of his grip and sprinted toward the theater.

"Oh God, not more running."

She laughed but didn't slow down. Despite his protest, she could hear the heavy jangling of his wallet chain start up again. She sped up, but only a little. He was far too exhausted to chase her down, and she didn't want to be too mean. She reached the theater while Rex remained at the far end of the rotunda, loping along slowly as his pants gradually slipped further and further down his narrow hips. She giggled as a strip of bright yellow boxer shorts appeared above his waistband.

Her laughter morphed into a shriek as a thunderous noise shook the building to its steely bones and the room plunged into darkness.

Chapter Seven

Mayhem, I'm coming! Stay there." Rex's voice echoed like there were ten of him as the jangle of his wallet chain increased in speed and volume. When he said her name again, it was from just a few feet away. "Are you alright?"

"Yeah, I'm fine," she said, tensing as his invisible fingers brushed her forearm. "What happened?"

"I can't say for sure, but I think the lights went out."

She scowled. "You can't see it, but I'm rolling my eyes."

"Yeah, I know."

They both yelped as a second metallic thud lit up the room with a dim, greenish glow.

"Ahhhh, okay," Rex said with a self-assured smile. "They probably turn off the main lights overnight. Nothing to freak out about."

Cari smiled. Under his nonchalance, there was a distinct tremble in his voice. "Either way, you're coming with me to get the blankets."

"For protection?"

"Yes. If there is a homicidal maniac running around, I wouldn't be able to live with myself if he killed you."

Rex swooned as he unlocked the movie theater. "My hero."

Cari waited in the lobby while he started the popcorn machine. "Let's make this quick," he said as they headed for Suttermill. "That thing is about a thousand years old and buggy as hell. It takes forever to warm up, and when it finally does, it goes from zero to Lake of Fire in three seconds flat."

"Why are they letting a minor operate something that dangerous?"

"They aren't. Not as far as they know."

She paused. "You lied on your application?"

Rex sighed and slid an arm over her shoulder. "I guess it's time you knew the truth. My name's not Drexel. It's Aladdin Matahari. And I'm not a high school freshman, I'm a post-graduate at Calbrion University Law School. So, whatever you do, don't fall in love with me. There's only one woman in my life, and that's sweet lady justice."

Cari pressed her lips together to keep from laughing. "It'll be hard, but I'll do my best."

With no lights and no inventory, traversing the empty shell that had once been Suttermill now felt like walking through a hollowed-out pumpkin three days after Halloween. At the back wall, they combed through refuse for something suitable, rifling through mismatched dish sets and kids' toys until they finally found a lime green king-sized quilt tucked in the corner. It was hideous, but it looked cozy and big enough for both of them.

"Did you really fill out your job application as Aladdin Matahari?" she asked as they retraced their steps back to the front of the store.

"Affirmative," he said, swinging the plastic case holding the quilt back and forth in a wide circle.

"And *nobody* questioned it?

"May, I've said it before, and I'll say it again: people in this town are idiots."

She chuckled. It was hard, if not impossible, to argue with that.

At they left Suttermill, she dug in her pocket for the store keys. Might as well lock up the nothing like she was supposed to, now that she had the time. She struggled the stiff metal gates in place and prepared to twist the key for the last time when a flicker of movement drew her attention to the army of unshod mannequins.

Smack in the middle of the blind, faceless horde, a magenta blouse shimmered beneath a mop of feathered blond hair.

Cari frowned, squinting in the dim green-hued light. "Holly?"

"What's that now?" Rex asked, briefly taking his eyes off the movie theater. Apparently, he was more concerned about the flammability of the popcorn machine than he let on.

"It's Holly," Cari returned as she slid back through the busted gates. They snagged shut the moment she cleared them. "She's…still here, I guess."

"Why?"

"How should I know?" Cari said exasperatedly. She rose to her tiptoes in an attempt to see around the dense thicket of plastic body parts. "Holly! It's me, Cari. What are you doing in there?"

Holly didn't answer. She didn't even move. A chill raced down Cari's spine. Carefully, she slid past the first row of mannequins toward her boss. "Holly? Holly, I swear to God, if this is a joke, it is not funny."

"Why do people always say that?"

Cari looked over her shoulder. Rex stood outside the security gate, his arms still wrapped around the Day-Glo quilt. "Say what?"

"In slasher movies, right before the person gets murdered, they always tell the murderer lurking in the shadows to quit messing around and, quote, this isn't funny. But who in their right might would joke-murder someone? That's how people get shot. Nope—nine times out of ten it's just a plain old murderer."

"Shut up, Rex," Cari grumbled, forcing her brain *not* to replay every horror movie where the dumb kid goes to investigate the creepy thing and ends up getting her head chopped off.

The further she went, the more packed-in the mannequins became, as if forming a protective circle around Holly. They're only plastic, she tried to tell herself. Hollow and light enough to knock over. So why was she bending and twisting to avoid even brushing against them?

As crazy as it sounded, she didn't want them to think she was rude.

Finally, she managed to sidle within arm's length of her target. Now she could hear something that had been too soft and far away for her to hear before—breathing, stuttered and brittle, like someone shivering in the cold. But Holly's form remained static, her arms pinned to her sides, her shoulders a solid line of pink against the darkness beyond her.

"Holly?" Cari ventured. She reached out, much as she had when she'd roused Holly from her doodle-fugue. Her fingers brushed the back of her silky blouse...

Holly pitched forward, toppling the mannequins in front of her like bowling pins. Cari yelped as they bounced against the linoleum in a massacre of dismemberments and projectile beheadings.

"What?" Rex yelled. "What's going on?"

"N-nothing! I mean…I-I don't know," she called back. Holly had done nothing to break her fall. Her arms hugged her sides as she lay face-down in a pile of plastic torsos. Except for the shallow rise and fall of her back, there was no movement to her at all.

Cari stooped low, and with timid, shaking hands, she grabbed Holly's shoulder. Her body felt warm, but rigid. Rolling her over was like trying to roll a log, but Cari didn't stop until Holly faced the ceiling. Her pink painted lips were slightly parted, her nostrils flaring ever so slightly, and—

Cari froze, her breath fleeing from her lungs. It couldn't be. She squeezed her eyes closed. Maybe it would disappear, the way it had before.

She opened her eyes.

Not this time. Both of Holly's eyes were still as black and slick as oil.

Holly's chest stopped moving. Her eyes and mouth opened wider and wider, stretching until it seemed the skin around them would snap. And the sound she made…like a pig being eviscerated between the grill of two semi-trucks. A gut-wrenching, inhuman screech.

"Christ on a cracker! What the hell *is* that?"

Somehow, Rex's voice cut through the noise. Grabbing onto his words like a life preserver, Cari fled. Plastic bodies flew in every direction as she scrambled toward the exit, manners now the furthest thing from her mind.

She yanked on the gate with every drop of her

adrenaline-fueled strength. It creaked and snapped encouragingly, but ultimately did not budge. She kept throttling it, unconcerned with anything but getting as far away from whatever the hell was going on in this store.

"We need to call an ambulance," she panted at Rex. "Or the police. We need—"

The pig noise cut out, the sudden silence freezing her mid-throttle. Turning slowly, she expected to see the black-eyed Holly bearing down on her.

All she saw was the decimated mannequin village. No monsters. No magenta blouse.

"Where'd she go?" Cari squinted into the pile of bodies. "Rex, did you see—?"

The words died in her throat. Standing behind a confused Rex was the largest, most hideous creature she had ever seen. A vaguely humanoid mass of mottled brown clumps, it towered at least three feet over Rex's five-ten and was about as wide as a car. Its arms were so long its knuckles dragging on the floor. From the top of its broad torso, a misshapen, featureless sphere drooped toward the unsuspecting boy below. If it weren't for the fact that it didn't have eyes, she would have thought it was watching him.

"Oh my God…"

At the sound of Cari's terrified whisper, the massive arms shot forward and wrapped themselves around Rex's waist.

"No!" She flung herself at the gate with renewed force. But after twenty-something years of abuse and neglect, the gate had apparently grown tired of being pushed around; no matter how hard she rattled or pried, it refused to move. "*Rex!*"

His only response was a strangled gurgle. The thing

hefted him off the ground as if he weighed no more than the quilt pressed into his chest. It began to squeeze. Rex's eyes bulged and his jaw sagged, but all he could manage was a short, harsh gasp. His face had turned the color of raw liver. Shaking from head to toe, Cari looked frantically from left to right, searching for…what? What could hurt it?

What the hell *was* it?

With a drunken groan, the thing's head recoiled into its shoulders like a turtle. A jagged line of what looked like raspberry jam appeared over the top of its skull as if it were grinning from ear to non-existent ear. With a wet pop, the line split like a Venus flytrap, revealing a crimson chasm spiked with row after row of broken yellow teeth.

Rex's eyes bulged even wider from their suffocating sockets, mouth open in a silent scream. And yet somehow, despite the certain destruction hovering right next to his ear, he managed to draw his gaze back to Cari. His hands and fingers twisted frantically in the air, unable to move any further under the weight of the gargantuan arms. Reaching for her. Begging her to do something. Save him.

Her fists slid helplessly down the metal gates.

"This can't be real." Her voice, but she hadn't said it. She couldn't have. She wasn't there. She was somewhere else, lost in grief and fear. Lost with him.

The thing's mouth sagged towards Rex. A snaggled tooth lacerated his forehead. Tears bathed her cheeks as the taste of iron flooded her throat.

She was about to watch her best friend die.

A loud splat shuddered her brain. Rex slipped to the ground, the left side of his head coated in a paste of raspberry jam and what looked a lot like mud. Cari's stomach lurched and her knees turned to water. Was that it? Was he dead? He must be. The thing had done whatever it had been trying to do.

And now it would come for her.

"Jesus…"

Rex inhaled the word with a dry, ragged breath. His eyes opened and found her almost immediately once again. The whites were webbed with red and his lips were almost purple, but he was alive. She exhaled for the first time what felt like years, unsure if the next breath would bring laughter or sobs.

It was neither. Instead, she screamed as the grotesque mass collapsed onto the floor next to Rex with a squishy thump. Where the pointy mouth had been was now nothing more than a slimy patch of what looked like bright red pumpkin guts streaked with chunky brown liquid. The only thing more disgusting than the look of it was the stench. It was as if that screaming pig from earlier had been left to rot on a sunbaked desert highway. And yet it barely registered. All she saw was Rex, alive, injured, and in need of help.

"Help!" she cried, rattling the stubborn gate. "If anyone is out there, please, somebody, help us!"

"Stand back."

A black hunk of metal came flying out of the shadows toward her. She jumped back as it struck the seam of the gate with an authoritative clang, then retreated into the darkness. Cari tested the gate. One side was still frozen up. The other, while still refusing to slide, had popped off its track far enough for her to bend it open and escape.

She fell to her knees, looping her arms under his and dragged him as far as away from the gruesome thing as she could manage. Coaxing the flattened quilt out from his arms, she slid it under his head like a pillow. "Are you okay?"

He smiled, his eyes opening and closing languidly. "Never better."

"Goddamn Creeps," came a voice from the shadows. "I just cleaned this floor too."

"So, clean it again. That's, like, eighty percent of your job, isn't it?"

Two voices. One woman, one man. And Cari recognized them both. From behind the impossible corpse emerged the pair she'd seen talking to Sam earlier that day. Grace and Cooper, she recalled, though their appearance had been slightly altered since that morning. Grace had tied the arms of her coveralls around her waist, revealing a tank top that might have been white once but was now streaked with a dull rainbow of stains. She wore a pair of brown suede workman's gloves and carried a sledgehammer at least three times larger than any Cari had seen before. Cooper had remained in his full security uniform, except now he'd added a black cargo vest, the pockets of which appeared to be quite full. In his right hand he held a long gun with a round magazine hanging below the stock. Both wore safety goggles, and neither seemed to be the least bit surprised by the giant monster oozing at their feet.

"You don't understand," Grace continued. "Whatever they make these bastards out of stains like a bitch. I literally have to go over the entire floor with bleach and a toothbrush to do a proper job."

"You could request better equipment."

She stared at him as if he had three heads. "And give Sam an excuse to lecture me on profit margin and solvency and whatever? Pass."

"Oh! I almost forgot." Cooper pulled a flat object wrapped in a wax paper bag out of his pocket. "For covering my shift last week. Allie's way of saying thank you."

Grace weighed the package suspiciously in her free hand.

"It's a cookie," Cooper supplied. "Peanut butter with chocolate drizzle. Her specialty."

"Not bad." She used her chin to nudge the package open. "Though you know that neither of you would have to thank me if you'd just hire a plumber."

"I'm married. I *am* a plumber. And an electrician, and a mechanic."

"Sounds like you need to unionize." She took a bite of the cookie. At their feet, the creature groaned. Without hesitating, Grace stomped a booted foot on the monster's back and dropped the business end of her hammer into the thing's misshapen skull. It made a sound like an underwater accordion as the last of its juices drained from its head. Cari watched the brown goop slither into the sunken grout between the cobblestones.

"Mm!" Grace exclaimed. "Not bad for peanut butter."

"What in the goddamn fucking *shit*?!"

Cari shrank back at Rex's roar. He rolled himself up and tried to stand. His shaken body had other ideas. Cari managed to wedge her shoulders under one of his arms before he collapsed completely.

Grace gave them a once-over, a bemused smile on her lips. "I think we're going to have to reverse direction on that, seeing as how, out of the four of us, Cooper and I are the only ones that are *supposed* to be here." She crossed her arms over the handle of her hammer. "We did last rounds at about ten to midnight and there was no sign of either of you. So! Who the hell are you, and what the hell are you doing here?"

Cari looked at Rex. He uttered a surly grunt before his head drooped forward dizzily.

Looked like she was on her own.

"Um, well…I'm Cari, and this is Drexel. Rex. I work…worked, at Suttermill, and I fell asleep in the back office, and I slept too long and then we were trying to leave but I had to get this…stuff for my mom, and—"

"Okay, okay. Honest mistake. Got it." Grace hefted the dripping hammer off of the monster's smashed head. "I'm Grace Henry, and this is Cooper. And this—" she nudged the beast with her foot "—is a Creep. That's what we call them, anyway. Don't know if they have a proper name. They're constructs, built out of dirt and rocks and shit and whatever else they can find. They make them big, strong, and stupid. Then they send them up here to…play."

Cari felt the hair on the back of her neck stand up. "Who's *they*?"

Grace glanced at Cooper, who tapped his watch.

"Later," she said. "We need to get you two somewhere safe. You obviously can't handle being out here on your own."

"Hey!" Rex said indignantly. "That thing got the jump on me. We could've wasted it if we'd known."

Cooper arched his eyebrow. "That's quite a statement coming from a kid who can barely stand."

"Dude, I'm not a kid. I'm sixteen. And as for the other thing…" Rex dropped his arm from Cari's shoulder and lurched forward. His knees looked ready to buckle again, but he kept himself up. "Eh? Pretty incredible, right?"

A loud, wet pop brought the conversation to an abrupt end It was quickly followed by a second, then a third.

"Uh," Cari groaned, her mouth as dry as lint. "Please tell me that's not what it sounds like?"

"'Fraid so." Gripping her hammer in both hands, Grace nodded at Rex. "Alright then, Mr. Incredible. We've seen you walk. Now let's see how good you run."

Chapter Eight

Cari's mind reeled. Was this really happening? Or was there a chance she was still asleep? She wanted to believe the latter so badly. But that noise assaulted her ears, wet and painful and undeniably real. She couldn't tell if the volume was because of increasing proximity or the number of creatures. Hopefully it wasn't both.

Something thumped against the back of her shoulder, not to injure but to spur movement. Turning, she saw Grace standing at her side.

"You can wrap your mind around it later," she said, grabbing the arm of her sweatshirt. "Right now, we've got to *move*!"

Grace yanked her forward, pulling her into a stumbling run. Next to her, Rex groaned as he forced his unsteady legs into yet another unwanted jog.

"No way we make it to the bunker!" Grace yelled to Cooper, who had assumed the lead.

"We gotta try!" he shouted over his shoulder. "We can't protect two civilians—two *kids*—against—"

His words petered out as a gargantuan creature emerged from under the arch. It was the same as the first one, inhumanly tall with a jellied mouth full of beige shards. Its deliberate steps shook the ground. Unlike the first, however, this guy hadn't come alone. Another behemoth plodded right behind him...and another, on and on until six behemoths crammed the mouth of the archway. Even at this distance, the smell was practically unbearable.

Cooper skidded to a halt. "Okay. No bunker." He turned to Grace. "Hi-Low. I'll take left, you take right."

"What about the kids?"

"They'll have to hide."

"Like hell we do!" Rex protested.

Grace ignored him. "Where?"

"How about the movie theater?" Cari supplied. She cocked her head toward the open doors.

"That'll work," Grace said. "Find a place with no windows and be as quiet as you can. If we don't...if they make it through, find something to throw at them. Sharp and heavy works best. Aim for their mouths if you can. Their bodies can be damaged, but they will regenerate. One good hit to the mouth will put 'em down ten times faster."

"Kind of like a video game," Cari said.

She raised her eyebrows in surprise. "Yeah, kind of like that." She lifted her hammer and looked at Cooper. "Ready?"

Cooper cocked his gun.

"Okay—*go!*"

Grace charged forward, screaming like a banshee at the advancing wall, while Cooper ran at full speed toward the fountain. He bounded over the lip of the basin and leaped upward, hooking his hands around the strongman's shoulders and scaling the statue like a monkey.

"I don't know about you, but this is *not* the chill

going-away party I had in mind," Rex quipped as Cari helped him limp into the movie theater as fast as he could. Once inside, he dropped to his knees. Her heart spluttered briefly but settled when she saw he was only fastening the doors floor lock. Even so, his hand shook so bad he could barely turn the bolt. He was trying so hard not to look afraid she didn't have the heart to point out that a single glass door was not going to provide much protection against those things, locked or otherwise.

"Okay, done," he said, using the door to help himself back to his feet. "Now what?"

"We can barricade ourselves in the projection booth," she suggested. "At least then we should be able to see them coming."

"Sounds solid to me."

They hadn't gone more than halfway across the lobby when the first ratchets of gunfire drew them back. Stationed on top of the marble globe, Cooper blasted away at the left side of the enemy line, slowly turning the giants into something that resembled a chocolate-strawberry shake. On the other side of the hall, Grace twirled her hammer like a baton, taking out a creature at its knee-like equivalent before delivering the death blow to its vulnerable face cavity as it writhed pitifully on the ground.

"They look like they have it under control," Rex said. But Cari heard the unmistakable tremble of doubt in his voice—the same doubt that had been rising in her own mind. Cooper and Grace could fight, no question. But the enemy line was still advancing; in the time it had taken Rex to lock the door, it had closed half the distance between the archway and the fountain. There were so many of them, and so few of Grace and

Cooper. It would only take one bite, one swipe to the leg, one hit to the head to turn the tables.

Rex cleared his throat. "So…you wanna hide?"

"Maybe." She arched an eyebrow at him. "You got a better idea?"

"Maybe." Grinning, he reached into his back pocket and extracted a slim paperback book. An image of an upside-down American flag dominated the tattered black cover.

"I knew it!" Cari exclaimed as Rex thumbed through the dog-eared pages. Another crackling blast from Cooper's gun made her wince.

"Hey, keep it down out there!" Rex yelled. "Can't you see I'm trying to read?"

Cari bounced on her knees impatiently, her gaze shifting from Rex to the ongoing battle. Working her way from right to left, Grace sprung from the mashed corpse of one Creep onto the shoulders of the next, wrapped her legs around the thing's fat neck, and plunged her weapon hilt-deep into the serrated mouth. It gagged as she twisted the handle and ripped it out, along with a huge chunk of the thing's throat. They'd almost gotten them all. Cari felt relief flood through her veins. Maybe they didn't need any help after all.

Then she saw a second line advancing out from the darkened archway. Only four this time, but still enough to drag her buoyed heart back to reality. *Of course,* it couldn't be that easy.

She turned back to Rex. His skimming had stopped on one of the last pages, which he was studying intensely. "I take it you found something?"

He clapped the book closed. "Nope. This book is total bullshit."

She frowned. "Then why do you look so happy?"

He cocked his chin at something over her shoulder. It didn't take long to see what he was referring to: the smoke was practically pouring out of the popcorn machine, the smell of burning oil so pungent she was a little embarrassed that she hadn't noticed it earlier.

"Okay," she said. "So…what are you thinking?"

His grin widened. "I'm thinking we should go bowling."

Chapter Nine

Cari pried the caps off the beer bottles with her keys and poured the contents down the sink, shaking each one vigorously to remove as much liquid as she could. Somewhere in the back of her mind, logic whispered sweet nothings in an attempt to rouse her sense of rationality. *This is crazy. This is impossible. This can't be happening. You're acting insane!*

She did her best to tell it to shut up. Insane or not, the danger certainly appeared to be real. If logic didn't want to help, it needed to stay the hell out of her way.

Meanwhile, Rex ransacked the entire kitchen to find what he needed—duct tape, a funnel, and a pair of thick rubber gloves. As soon as she set an empty bottle on the counter Rex swiped it up and placed it under the crackling popcorn hopper. With one gloved hand and a delicate touch, he tipped the hopper. A thin stream of bubbling brown liquid dribbled into the bottle.

"That gun of Cooper's," Rex said as he grabbed another empty. "Do you think that's an actual AA-12?"

"A what?"

"It's a kind of shotgun. Full auto. It's military-grade assault weaponry."

"Sounds illegal," she murmured, shaking the last

bottle dry.

"Oh, it's *very* illegal. That's my point. AA-12s are not exactly standard issue for rent-a-cops, especially at a mall on life support. How the hell does *that* guy have one?"

Cari snapped on her own pair of gloves and took one of the bottles gingerly by the neck. Even through the rubber she could feel the heat of the bottle as she sealed the mouth with a square of duct tape. "If I had to guess, I'd say it's probably to deal with all the monsters."

"Fair point." He jiggled the hopper to drain it of its last drops of oil. "That's it. Three and a half bottles."

"Do you think it's enough?"

"*Grace!*"

Cooper's terrified shout tore through the air, prompting both Cari and Rex to race for the entrance. Cooper remained on top of the fountain, in the process of ejecting his clip and grabbing a fresh one from one of his vest pockets. Two Creeps remained on the left side of the hall, still on their feet and approaching in long, slow strides. On the right side, Grace swept the hammer over her head, preparing to drop it into the face of the Creep gnashing its teeth on the ground below her. Her hammer had already smashed its legs to pudding, but that hadn't stopped it from wrapping a massive hand around Grace's calf.

"Son of a bitch," Rex exhaled. "That thing's gonna bite right through her."

But Grace wasn't going down without a fight. Steadying herself on her free foot, she adjusted her grip until she held her weapon like a golf club. The hammer sliced through the air and landed with a spine-tingling crack in the middle of the giant fist. The thing screamed.

And so did Grace. She collapsed to the ground, clutching her now free but smashed shin, the pain blinding her to the monster lingering close by, alive and seething at her.

"Looks like we're up. Here." Rex handed a bottle to Cari. "Your aim has always been better than mine."

"Okay," she said, blushing slightly at the compliment. She unlocked the door while Rex retrieved the other three bottles. "Ready?"

He clinked the bottles together. "Ready and waiting."

She threw the doors open and ran forward at full tilt, sliding to a stop in front of the fountain. Twenty feet away, Grace lay on her back in a slick of monster goo, still too out of it to see the impending destruction looming over her. The thing had practically ripped its own skull in half at the prospect of sinking its teeth into her.

The bottle shook in Cari's hand. If she misjudged the distance, she would hit Grace. It would hurt. She would have scars.

But that was better than being ripped to shreds by a hell giant, right?

She inhaled and pulled her arm back. A burst of breath, and she let it fly.

"*Incoming!*" Rex bellowed.

Grace didn't move. Above Cari, Cooper looked up from struggling with his weapon and saw the bottle arching through the air. "Grace, cover!"

She snapped into a fetal position without hesitation. The bottle landed smack in the middle of the Creep's back and shattered. It roared like a gutted grizzly as the boiling oil gouged deep rivers into its swampy flesh, thrashing its arms as if trying to fend off the attack. Grace scrambled out of the way before a flailing boulder of a fist could further crush her injured leg. At last, the Creep collapsed into a smoking, deflated lump.

"Another!" Cari held out her hand. Rex slapped a second bottle into her palm. This time she aimed for the two remaining Creeps on the left, the ones still on their feet.

It landed between them. Droplets of oil sprayed their legs.

They barely flinched.

"Dammit," Cari grumbled. "Another!"

This time she targeted the rightmost Creep's torso. A direct hit. The thing let out a long wheeze, like someone who had been punched in the gut. As planned, the bottle broke.

Then it exploded.

"Shit!" she screeched as the Creep disappeared inside a pillar of flames. "How did *that* happen?"

"Who *cares*? That freak is on fire!" Rex thrust the last bottle into her hands and bolted back to the movie theater before she could ask where the heck he thought he was going. Above her, Cooper's magazine finally clicked into place. Taking deliberate aim, he nudged the trigger and fired a single round into the mouth of the burning Creep. It staggered and fell—straight into the Creep next to it.

Shouldering his gun, Cooper stepped off the globe, casually dropping the ten feet to the ground. He landed next to Cari as the second Creep joined its comrade in a fiery death.

"One side, people!" Rex streaked past them, wobbling under the weight of what appeared to be a bag of unmixed concrete. He tossed the grainy white contents over the blaze, subduing the flames.

"How did you do that?" Cari asked, surprised—and, if she had to admit it, impressed.

Rex held up the half-empty bag so she could read the label. *Commercial Popcorn Salt. 50 lbs.*

"You don't have hobbies like mine without learning a thing or two about fire safety," he said as he dropped the bag onto the floor. "You're welcome."

"Seeing how you started the fire, I'm not sure thanks should be necessary," Grace said as she joined their circle, leaning on the handle of her hammer like a cane. She was covered in dark sludge and smelled like she'd swam fifty laps in an Olympic-sized Porta-Potty. Compared to the stink of the room at large, however, her individual odor barely registered.

Cooper nodded at Grace's shin. "Bad?"

"It's certainly not good," she said.

Then Cari noticed the puckered red wounds streaked across Grace's forearms and chest.

"Oh my God. Did I hit you?"

Grace looked down at her arms. "Huh, will you look at that? I didn't even notice."

"You didn't notice a grease burn?" Rex frowned. "What's wrong with you?"

She glared at him. "Oh, I'm sorry. I was a little distracted by the giant monster trying to kill me, you, and everyone in the room. My bad."

A crackle of static made them all jump.

"Team Selene, report," demanded a distorted, static-ridden voice.

"It's about time," Cooper muttered as he unclipped a chunky hand radio from his belt. "Selene here. Where have you guys been?"

"Sorry, Coop. A Maw opened right outside the bunker and

it interfered with the signal. Team Helios jumped on it ASAP but took heavy damage and had to return to base. Maybe if you'd circled back—"

"If *we'd* circled back?!" Grace yanked the radio to her mouth, prompting a grunt from Cooper. "Did you see what we've been dealing with out here? Where was *our* backup?"

"Um, well...like I said, the signals were interrupted, so the cameras have all been out too. I'm rebooting the system now."

Grace snorted. "You mean you unplugged it and plugged it back in."

"Uh, yeah, basically. It should be up in another half a minute or so. Okay? I promise. Stand by."

The stuttering voice cut out.

"You shouldn't yell at him like that," Cooper said. "You know he's got anxiety issues."

"What's the point of having a head of surveillance if he doesn't help you when you need him?" she shot back.

"Wait a minute," Cari said. "You mean there's more to this than you two?"

Grace and Cooper exchanged a questioning look, as if trying to determine who should say what. Before they could decide, the radio crackled again.

"Cameras coming back online. One more second and...oh good God."

"My thoughts exactly," Grace said.

"You're on the live feed?" Cooper asked.

"Affirmative."

"Then in addition to the mess, you can see that we've made some new friends." Cooper pointed to the top of one of the rotunda's columns and the intermittent red blink of a security camera. "Say hi, kids."

Cari waved sheepishly at the camera. Rex cocked two finger guns.

"Shit," the radio squeaked.

"Yes, Simon. I think we've pretty well covered that the situation is shit," Grace said.

"No, not—well, yes, that, but we've got a bigger problem. It looks like there's another Maw forming."

Something in the radio's tone made Cari's scalp squirm. Cooper must have felt it too; when he spoke again, his voice was grave. "Where?"

The entire room began to shake. For one fanciful moment, Cari allowed herself to think it was an earthquake. Nothing supernatural, just a nice, normal danger that could be defended by ducking in a doorway and waiting for it to pass. Then she saw the air on the opposite side of the fountain in front of Ripped! Fitness start to...the only word she could think of was *throb*. It was as if someone had stretched plastic wrap over the entrance and was intermittently pulling on the edges of it, expanding and contracting the facade in even, steady pulses. With every expansion, the center of it grew a little darker, until the entire doorway was nothing more than a big purple bruise suspended in space.

Cooper groaned. "Ripped again? That's the third time this month."

Grace shrugged. "That's Creeps for you. Big, strong, and stupid."

A metallic screech made them all cover their ears as a shaft of crimson light punched through the middle of the shadow like a red-hot machete.

"Take cover!" Grace shouted, hobbling into a crouch with her back against the fountain. Cari joined her, followed by Rex. The floor vibrated beneath her palms as the crack in the shadow widened. Now she could see things moving on the other side. Big things. Tentacled things.

Evil things.

"Selene, come in. We've got problems. Helios is out of commission, and the Doc is gearing up but... shit, guys, I think you're gonna have to figure this one out on your own."

"Great pep talk, Simon. You should coach little league." Grace snapped. She peered over the rim of the fountain. "It's not fully formed yet. Can we take it out before it stabilizes?"

Cooper studied the thickening blade of light. "Maybe. But I've only got the one magazine left. Bullets alone would take three full clips, even when it's at half strength. Maybe if we had something extra. Something with...a blast radius."

Cari felt their eyes zero in on the last bottle, still clenched in her fist.

Grace cocked her head at Cooper. "Hm?"

"Hm," he answered. "Yeah. Worth a shot, anyway."

"Roger that." Grace turned to Cari. "Can you hit it?"

Cari gaped at her. "Me? Uh, I, um...I don't know..."

"Let me put this another way," Grace cut her off. "My leg's busted, Cooper's basically tapped out, and this kid is...also here. If you don't hit that target, they are going to kill us, break out of here, and then...then things get really bad. So, I'm going to ask you again. Can. You. Hit. It?"

Cari looked from Grace to the bottle. It pulsed warm in her handle, bubbling with unleashed firepower. She *was* two for three. But the second one had been way off, and the first one, though a hit, had been off kilter enough to splash Grace. And those things had been *huge*. The…Maw, or whatever it was called, clocked in at half their size at best. Not to mention that, if Cooper really planned to shoot it in midair, the timing needed to be perfect.

A second shearing growl roared through the air, making the floor tremble violently. Grace yelped as she lost her balance and collapsed into her bad leg.

"It's getting stronger," Cooper said. "If we're gonna do this, it has to be now."

Cari's eyes darted from Cooper back to Grace, her face scrunched in pain, and finally to Rex. He knelt on all fours next to Grace, and while his face was composed, his eyes were glassy with fear.

"It's only half full," Cari said softly.

"I know." His eyes ticked up toward the glowing perforation. The red light danced across the marble floor like sunlight through stained glass. "But I think I've had enough fun for one night. Don't you?"

She giggled despite her nerves. "I think if I have any more, it'll kill me."

She shot Grace a look—more of a question, really—that she hoped the older woman would understand. Grace's bobbed her head once in response. After Cari turned away, she heard scuffling behind her as Grace dragged Rex back toward the entrance of the movie theater. She breathed a sigh of relief. Crouching by the edge of the fountain, she nodded to Cooper. "Let's do it."

"10-4." He tucked the stock of the gun to his shoulder so the scope was level with his eye. Cari followed its trajectory. The ragged hole hung suspended three feet in the air, about fifteen feet away.

Or was it eighteen?

"Ready?"

She bit her lip, unable to answer such a ridiculous question. Of course she wasn't ready. Who in world *would* be?

Another tremble buzzed through the floor. Unlike the previous tremors, this was softer, subtle, almost pleasant.

Why did that make it so much more terrifying?

"Cari?" Cooper prodded.

Ready or not, something was coming.

She gripped the bottle by the neck and nodded. "Ready."

"Aim."

She inhaled, letting her arm hang back as she crouched on the balls of her feet.

"Fire!"

She sprang up like a jackrabbit. The red light stung her skin like a swarm of angry hornets. Her arm shook, then locked. Now that she had a full, unobstructed view into the portal and the things on the other side, she could see that they were…not so bad. Not so bad at all. The light wasn't red, but the brilliant gold of a sunny sky. And the big things were not monsters, but trees. Beautiful, lush trees with velvety blue flowers that somehow, she knew would smell like jasmine. And the tentacled things were not tentacles. They were vines that led up to the giant trees where happy little squirrels and birds and butterflies frolicked to no end.

She stumbled as her front foot slid a few inches forward. There was a place for her there. She felt that keenly. She would be welcome. She could leave this town and this world and this life behind her. She could escape for good. She would never have to feel alone or scared or unhappy ever again.

Her back foot wobbled, aching to move as well. She

vaguely heard someone calling her name, but it was secondary. Then tertiary. Then a total non-issue. All that mattered was the light, and the beautiful, horrible things inside it.

Mayhem…

The word tickled the back of her neck. She shook her head, trying to drive it away. Instead it dug in deeper and brought the rest of the world crashing in with it.

"—now! Mayhem! Throw it *now!*"

She shook her head, and the spell dissipated. Squinting her eyes against the hypnotic light, she pulled her arm back and shot it forward, releasing the bottle at the top edge of the arc. All sound fell away as she watched the bottle sail end-over-end toward its target.

She undershot it.

Or wait…no, she overshot it.

Or maybe…

The bottle dropped into the direct center of the Maw.

"Yes!" She punched the air.

A mountainous arm shot out from the void, wrapping the bottle in its thick, rocky fingers.

She dropped her hand. "Oh, come *on!*"

"Cari, get down!"

She flopped onto her stomach and covered her head as Cooper let loose at the clenched fist. Small divots appeared in the surrounding floors and walls, but both the fist and the Maw seemed unaffected.

"It's a Gladiator!" Cooper growled in frustration. "The skin's too thick, I can't penetrate."

"Hold your fire!" Grace yelled from inside the movie theater, her arm still wrapped around Rex's neck. "It's gonna move. It has to. Wait."

Cooper complied. Sure enough, the hand with the bottle was followed by a shoulder, and then a head. But this one was different. Instead of a blind mouth, this one had eyes—if the two purple-veined, ventricle-strapped lumps pulsing in craggy sockets could be considered eyes. But eyes or hearts or something else, they didn't survive for long. With a frustrated roar, Cooper unloaded at them with the last of his arsenal. The creature reeled back, losing its grip on the bottle as it did. The gun clicked empty, but not before the bottle exploded in a torrent of glass, oil, rocks, and goop. The edges of the Maw spasmed, then snapped, vivisecting what was left of the now-faceless Gladiator. The building shivered from the impact before settling into a silence as cold and deep as a grave.

"Nice arm."

Cari turned around. Grace wasn't smiling, but the soft glow in her dark eyes made her look slightly less annoyed.

"Thanks," Cari said. She had barely regained her balance when Rex swooped in and wrapped her in a big hug.

"That was amazing!" he crowed, swinging her like a child swinging his teddy bear. "I said you had the best aim. Didn't I say it?"

"Yes, you did. Now put me down," Cari squealed until he released her. "I promise I'll never make fun of you being a total psycho anarchist ever again."

"*Outstanding!*" The radio whooped on Cooper's belt. "*We're gonna have to remember that trick. What on Earth do they keep in that theater? Dynamite?*"

"Not recently," Rex said under his breath. Cari elbowed him in the ribs. If she could barely tell when he was being serious, how could they?

"We're clear out here, Simon," Cooper radioed back. "You see any more activity?"

"Nope, we're all good. Come on in."

"Roger that. Over and out." Cooper clipped the radio back onto his belt. "Let's try this again, shall we?"

Chapter Ten

They picked their way through the swampy muck and body parts with Cooper in the lead and Grace bringing up the rear, struggling to slide the head of her hammer-slash-cane over the uneven ground.

As Cari surveyed the carnage, each step grew heavier and harder to take. This was nothing like a theme park or a video game. This was *real*. Monsters were real. Hell—if that's what that place had been—was real.

What was she supposed to *do* with all that?

"Everything okay up here?"

Cari tipped her head up as Grace fell in step with her. "Yeah...well, I mean, no. Not really." She shook her head. "How could I have missed this? I've been working here since June, and I never even...how could I not notice?"

"Because you weren't supposed to," Grace said. "We spend a lot of time and energy making sure people don't notice. I wouldn't lose too much sleep over it."

"Yeah, May," Rex said. "I've worked all over this dump for two years and I didn't notice anything either."

Cari smirked. "Yeah, but you're kind of an idiot."

Rex chucked her on the chin. "You're so sweet to me."

Grace groaned. "Jeez, get a room why don't you?"

Cari burst out laughing. A few seconds later, Rex joined her. The thought was too ridiculous to take seriously.

They reached the arch. Cooper held up his hand indicating they should wait. He leaned around the corner, took a quick look in both directions, then waved them forward.

"Grace, take the lead. I'll cover you. Make sure nothing's on our tail."

"What's wrong?" Grace asked, sliding further forward. "You think we forgot something?"

Chk-chk-chk-chk-chk.

They all froze. Somewhere in the carnage behind them, a quiet skittering punctured the stillness.

"What the hell was that?" Rex hissed.

"I don't know," Cooper said, turning his empty gun in his hand until he held it like a baseball bat. Shifting as much weight as she could to her good leg, Grace dragged her hammer off the ground with a soft, pained grunt.

Chk-chk-chk-chk-chk.

The same noise. Louder. Closer. And undeniably up.

Did we forget something? Cari repeated the question as they slowly shifted into a back-to-back circle. *Did we forget something...*

The realization hit her like a bucket of ice.

"Rex?"

"Yeah?"

"We *did* forget something." She curled her fingers into the sleeve of his t-shirt, struggling to keep her voice steady. "We forgot about Holly."

A skin-shriveling screech shattered the silence. All eyes drew up as the black-eyed thing that used to be Holly flung itself off the balcony. Stunned and frozen in both movement and thought, Cari could only watch as her former boss plunged toward her, arms extended and fingers curled into claws. Her cracked lips split into a joker smile punctuated by slick, stained teeth.

"Everybody belly flop!"

She didn't have to be told twice. Her chest hit the stones as the air above her exploded. She looked up in time to see Holly fly smash into the far wall, her body crumbling to the floor like a bag of sticks. In the ringing silence that followed, Cari searched the room for the person to whom she owed her physical non-deformity, if not her life.

When she found him, standing in front of the east entrance, she recognized him immediately. It was impossible not to—she saw him every day. Now, with the smoking shotgun in his hands and a cold sneer on his face, he looked less like Santa Claus and more like Santa's mobbed-up twin. Saint Nicky Scarface.

"John?" Cari whispered.

His sneer disappeared as his eyes crinkled into a smile. He lowered the gun. "Indeed. A pleasure as always...Cari, right?"

"Yeah." She was as surprised by his recall as she was about the gun.

"Dammit, John!" Grace limped up to him, sounding more incensed than she had all night. "That was an assimilated you just shot. Now we have a whole other kind of mess to clean up."

"You would rather I let her rip into you like she did poor Mr. Jackson?"

"No," Grace sighed, her anger losing some of its edge. "How is Charlie anyway?"

"Doing well, all things considered. Out of surgery and doing quite well I'm told. A week or two in the hospital and he'll be good as new. Except for the eye, of course."

"Well…good. I'll be sure to send flowers. In the meantime, what are we supposed to tell people when *this* one doesn't show up for work?" She jerked her head in Holly's direction.

"She doesn't work here anymore." Cari piped in. "She was my boss at Suttermill. Today was her…our…last day."

"There, you see?" John said. "Nothing to worry about. Besides—"

Across the hall, Holly groaned and rolled onto her back. Cari shrank behind Rex at the sight of the two-dozen tiny, bleeding wounds scattered over Holly's cheeks and chest.

"She's fine." He patted his gun. "Loaded it with birdshot. Disarms and injures, but rarely kills."

Grace shook her head. "Risky move, Boss."

"This isn't my first rodeo." He extended his hand to Cooper. "Lieutenant O'Bannon, if you would be so kind?"

Cooper sighed. "Is that really necessary?"

"If we want to get her down to the bunker without incident, it is."

Cooper trudged over to the groaning woman, suspended the gun stock down above her temple, and dropped it with a cringeworthy crack. The groaning ceased. Slinging the gun onto his back, Cooper hefted the unconscious Holly in his arms.

"Thank you," John said. "You can put her in Cell

One. I'll assess her there and see if there's anything we can do for her other than the obvious."

"The obvious?" Cari asked.

"You know." Grace pointed a finger at her temple and snapped her thumb down.

"Oh." Cari looked at her feet, embarrassed. That *was* pretty obvious.

John led the way past the east entrance, down a short hallway that ended at the mouth of a sporting goods store. Instead of proceeding all the way to the locked gates, he veered left through a narrow archway that led to the restrooms. Halfway down the hall two sets of plain gray double doors faced each other. John opened the doors on the left, with the words Security Staff Only written in peeling black paint. The set on the right was labeled simply Maintenance.

Inside, Cari recognized the arched window of the greeter's desk, only now she was looking at it from the inside out. On the opposite wall were three grainy closed-circuit televisions and a tall filing cabinet, on top of which stood the solicitous little elf John had acquired earlier in the day. It might have been cute except that he was backward, the tails of his green jacket facing out as he offered his gift to the wall.

"This is the bunker?" Cari asked.

"Sort of," John said. "Three exterior cameras might be enough to satisfy our friends at corporate, but our purposes require something a bit more robust. Luckily, Ray was good enough to allow my input regarding the renovation this place underwent seven years ago. I managed to slip in a few little upgrades underneath the new paint." He slid open the second drawer of the cabinet. Instead of files, it contained a keypad. He punched a series of numbers, then stepped back as the cabinet swung out to the left, revealing a descending staircase. Except for a faint blue glow, Cari couldn't see the bottom. Now the elf made sense—with the cabinet swung out, he could now greet all those brave enough to venture down the stairs.

"Does Sam know about this?"

"No," Grace said testily, "and he's never going to."

"Why not?"

"Because knowing him, he'd probably want to charge admission."

Cooper descended the steps first, angling his body to avoid knocking Holly's head into the cement wall. Grace approached next, but John stepped in to block her way.

"What happened there?" He pointed at her leg.

Grace looked sheepish. "I had to smash it."

His gray eyebrows rose. "You *had* to smash it? There wasn't any other option?"

She raised her chin defiantly. "Tell you what. Next time a Creep is about to turn me into a human juice box, I'll tell him to hold up until you have the chance to weigh in. Besides, it's not even broken."

He struggled to suppress a smile. It would only encourage her. "How can you be sure?"

"I know what a broken bone feels like."

"Yes, I know you do," he sighed. "Go the med station. I'll check it after I finish assessing the convert."

Grace rolled her eyes. Her attention fell back to Cari and Rex. "What do we do about them?"

He studied them, rubbing his chin thoughtfully as a plan began to form. Not a grand plan, but certainly an obvious one. "Our best fixer *is* in the hospital, and the rotunda *is* covered in liquefied Creep. Seems like we could use a few extra hands."

Grace frowned. "They're awfully young."

"Maybe. But they saved your bacon tonight, didn't they?"

She shook her head. As much as she tried to appear stern, he spotted a subtle hint of something other than irritation behind her eyes. If he didn't know better, he'd said it was pride.

"It's your call, Boss," she said at last.

"Thank you, Ms. Henry." He stepped aside. "Off you go."

Grace disappeared down the stairs, leaving Cari and Rex along with John. He continued to study them, his jovial face growing more serious until he was nearly scowling. Cari felt her shoulders tighten in anticipation of an outburst.

Instead, he sighed and lowered his eyes to the ground.

"I'm sorry," he said softly. "I'm sorry you got pulled into this, and that you can't unsee what you saw tonight. But more than that, I'm sorry that what you saw is the tip of an extremely dangerous iceberg."

He extended his hand to Cari. She was dazed enough to accept it. He shook her hand warmly, then offered the same to Rex. "Welcome to Virgil Security and Maintenance. I hope you two know your way around a mop."

He began to descend the stairs.

"Wait!" Cari called after him.

He paused but didn't turn more than his head. "Yes?"

"Why…why is this happening?"

John's entire posture shifted once again, this time

becoming as cold and hard as granite. "Because even good people can make bad decisions."

Cari's lower lip quivered. She wanted to say something, to address the huge, horrible emotions lurking below the surface, but she couldn't find the words.

"Now what the hell does *that* mean?"

Good thing Rex always did. She smiled at the ground as he threw up his hands in disgust. "I swear to God, I've had it up to here with the cryptic language and significant glances. If someone doesn't give us a straight answer soon, I'm seriously gonna lose it."

John blinked, the cordial smile returning. "Young man, I'm afraid the straight answer isn't always the short answer. Stick around, and I promise, you'll hear it all."

He retreated down the stairs.

Rex snorted. "Can you believe the balls on that guy? Assuming we'd join their weird little club without even *asking* us first?"

"Yeah, totally lame," Cari agreed. It *was* pretty arrogant. And yet the longer they stood there, the more she found herself drawn to the secret door and its cool, comforting light.

"Although…"

"Yeah?" Cari turned to Rex. She was relieved to see he was still pondering the door too.

"Well, tonight *was* pretty fun," he continued. "And we did kick a lot of ass."

She snorted. "Oh yeah, it was lots of fun. Remember the part where you almost died? That was awesome."

Rex held up a finger. "*That* doesn't count. Like I told you before, I wasn't ready."

"Sure, keep telling yourself that," she said with a wink, trying to keep the tone light even though the memory of it made her want to throw up.

He rolled his eyes. "My point is, under the right circumstances, I could see us doing more of...whatever this is."

Cari nodded. "Yeah. Me too."

"Cool. In that case..." He extended his hand toward the door. "After you."

She was about to step forward when her body began to vibrate. She let out a shriek.

"What?!" Rex whipped one way and the other, his arms drawing back in a ninja attack stance. "What is it?"

"I don't...oh," She withdrew her buzzing cell phone from her pocket. Rex's shoulders relaxed, but only a little. She didn't have to check the caller ID to know who it would be.

"Don't answer it," he said.

Cari stared at the shaking metal square. "I have to." She flipped the phone open.

"Yes, Mother?"

"Cury..."

No over-enunciation this time. The syllables were so soft and wet they barely resembled a word. Guilt gnawed at her heart.

This is my fault. I did this.

"Wur the hell ur my cig'rettes? I've been so usset all day, and you wur sposed ta get um an—"

I did this, didn't I?

Or did I?

"I need um anni need the recrown an—"

"Get it yourself."

The words were out of Cari's mouth before she realized she was speaking. Rex's jaw dropped as her mother's drunken spluttering filled her ear.

"Whu the—"

"You heard me," Cari said, her heart racing like a steam engine as her mouth gained speed. "If you want to drink yourself stupid, fine. I don't *care* anymore. But I'm not going to help you do it. If you need beer, or cigarettes, or condoms for your nasty two-timing hypocrite boyfriend, you can drive your own *ass* down here to the Buck Stop and get them yourself! I'll even help you out."

She hurled the phone out the guest relations window as hard as she could.

"Jesus!" Rex cried as it snapped in half against the far wall. "What the hell was *that?*"

"It had to be done," Cari said, slightly out of breath. "Otherwise she'd have kept calling."

Rex nodded. For a moment neither of them spoke. They simply stood side by side, staring out the window at the pieces of Cari's destroyed phone scattered across the cobblestones of the East Hall.

"She's gonna kill you," Rex said at last.

"She can try," she said, sounding spiteful and meaning it for once. She knew he might be right. Maybe her mother would retaliate. And so what if she did? Cari had faced death tonight and won. She could do it again. And again. She'd do it a thousand times if she had to. But that was a problem for another time. Right now, in this moment, she felt better than she had in years.

Taking a deep, satisfied breath, she turned to Rex. Even though they hadn't left each other's side for more than a few minutes all night, Cari felt like she hadn't seen him in ages. His eyes were still bloodshot, his face and clothes caked in all manner of gunk. There were new lines etched around his mouth and forehead, either from shock or trauma or plain old exhaustion. She knew his face better than she knew her own almost, and it looked as though it had aged ten years.

"Ready?" She held out her hand.

He grabbed it and threaded his fingers with hers. "Ready and waiting."

Together, they walked through the door.

Acknowledgments

The *Dead Mall* series would not have been possible without the time and support of numerous people. Big thanks go out to my critique partner Jeff; my Sin City Writers Group (especially Toni, Terri, Melissa, Jason, Diana, and Kurt); my editor, Jami; and my husband, Marcin, who suffered through the early drafts so you didn't have to.

Thank you as well to William Burleson for sharing his knowledge of business things; to Scott Burtness for his insights into the world of indie publishing; and to Fran and Erica for their endless quest to purge my work of extraneous commas.

Finally, a huge thanks to Joseph Reedy, illustrator-slash-genius. Thanks for putting up with me!

Please consider rating or reviewing it on Amazon or Goodreads. To order the other Dead Mall books or to receive updates about new releases, visit www.sgtasz.com.

IF YOU ENJOYED *WELCOME TO HALCYON*,
DON'T MISS THIS EXCERPT FROM THE
THRILLING CONTINUATION OF
THE DEAD MALL SERIES:

PART II: VEILED THREATS

They jogged past the greeter's desk, the arched bridge, and the abandoned shell of a Mrs. Field's Cookies until they reached the ragged perforation hovering at the far end of the East Hall. Simon hadn't been exaggerating—even partially formed, the Maw was already as big as an elephant, its semi-transparency staining the midnight mosaic behind it a rotten-plum brown. Cari kept her eyes pinned to the back of Grace's head. The last time she'd looked directly into a Maw, she'd frozen up. That wouldn't happen again. Whatever abomination awaited them this time, she was not going to give it the benefit of her hesitation.

As if sensing their approach, the droopy Maw snapped into a taut circle of swirling red light. Grace gripped her hammer like a baseball bat while at the front, A.J. reached into the folds of his coat and unsheathed two short flat-bladed swords. Despite her nerves, Cari smiled appreciatively. Storing both pistols and a pair of mini-katanas on his belt was a feat of fashion engineering the likes of which she had never seen. It certainly backed up Grace's claim that he was truly a team of one.

A keening moan sliced through the hall. The light constricted like a pupil in the sun before flooding the

Maw with deep, black nothing. Setting her feet in a pitcher's stance, Cari gripped the bottle and braced herself for the phalanx of monsters that was about to come marching out.

Instead, a small bundle of brown fur tumbled out of the depths and landed with a plop and a whine on the gray cobblestones.

"What the hell?" Rex muttered, voicing her confusion as well as his own. They leaned forward to get a better to look. A small brown ball of fur huddled near the base of the Maw, blinking its yellow eyes and whimpering in distress.

Cari frowned. Was that a kitten?

Her confusion was compounded as several more fluffy little fuzzballs emerged, tabbies and calicoes and even a teeny tiny Scottish fold. With each arrival, the edges of the Maw blurred and receded, until only the motley litter remained, stumbling and mewling in precious disorientation.

"Awww," Rex cooed, edging past Cari toward the pile. "Look at 'em. They're so—"

A blast of compressed air cut him off as a fine mesh net descended on the kittens, quickly entangling itself in their uncoordinated limbs. Cari whipped her head toward A.J., who shoved the net gun back into the arsenal on his back. With a sweep of his hands, he scooped the net off the ground, trapping the squirming brood in a translucent makeshift sack.

"Why'd you do that?" Cari was startled to hear her own voice, yelling at a man with the backpack full of guns. "They're just kittens."

He looked at her as if he hadn't even noticed her standing there until now. His eyebrows drew together beneath the shadow of his hat. "Kittens? You think so?"

Without waiting for her answer, he wound up and smashed the sack against the floor in a symphony of thunks, crunches and heart-wrenching yowls.

"No!" she shrieked.

But A.J. continued to smash. The bottle slipped from her fingers and smacked against the cobblestones as she clamped her hands over her face. Two hits became three, and then more, until it sounded like a wet towel being flapped against the ground. She choked back a sob, chasing away visions of what the poor things must look like now.

"Christ, man, isn't that enough?" Rex said. He was doing his best to sound gruff, but she could hear the waver in his voice. At last, the horrible noise stopped.

"Look now," A.J. said, slightly out of breath.

Cari shook her head, pressing her palms to her tearing eyes. Her imaginings had been bad enough. She didn't need to see it for real.

She jumped as something brushed her elbow.

"It's okay." Cooper's voice this time, as soft and comforting as a down quilt. "It's not what you think. Trust me."

His tugged gently at her arm. Shaking, she relented. Dark liquid smeared the cobblestones. She was about to cover her eyes again, or possibly vomit, when she noticed the color. She squinted at the stain, leaning forward ever so slightly to make sure she was seeing it right. Sure enough, the liquid wasn't red, but a deep purplish black.

"What the…?" Taking a deep breath, she coaxed her eyes toward the mangled mass suspended from A.J.'s fist—and recoiled instantly. Instead of kittens, the smashed-up carcasses of a dozen basketball-sized spiders hung ensnared in the nylon netting. Between their size and the leathery blue-green plates covering their bodies, they looked more like dinosaurs than bugs. All of them were shattered, and most of them were dead. The few that remained glared venomously at A.J with faceted yellow eyes, their broken limbs twitching as they gnashed at the air with long, slick teeth.

"Oh, my God." Cari covered her mouth. Bile burned the back of her throat again as a series of different visions floated through her mind. She saw herself reach down to scratch behind a fuzzy kitten ear, and then its jaws opened, and its teeth…

She shook her head. If it hadn't been for A.J., she would have lost a hand.

Rex looked just as shaken. He stared at the bag, eyes perfectly round, one hand buried nervously in his hair. "Why would they do that?"

"To send a message," Cooper said. "A little hello to the new kids on the block."

"How thoughtful," Rex said bitterly. "Maybe we should get something for them. Like a fruit basket full of scorpions."

"I wouldn't recommend it," Grace said. "But I like the enthusiasm."

She lifted her hammer as A.J. set the bag on the ground. One of the few survivors flopped onto its back, squealing and spitting purple blood as Grace approached. Its barb-tipped feet scraped against the stone as it tried to right itself, but it was no use—too many of its legs were broken.

"Word of advice, kids," Grace said, "Never underestimate anything that comes out of a Maw. No matter how cute or appealing it looks, it's all the same nightmare underneath."

She raised her weapon. Once again, Cari averted her eyes. She was by no means sad to hear the hammer come down, and yet she couldn't help wincing a little at the thick, wet crunch.

"All Teams, report."

Cooper unhooked the radio from his belt. "We're clear, Specs. They popped a Trojan horse, but we neutralized it."

A.J. arched an eyebrow. "We?"

"Correction. Helios neutralized it. And the Maw appears to have disintegrated on its own."

"Um…are you sure? The heat sensors are still picking up activity in the area. Looks like there's another one out there."

Cari swiveled her head up and down the hall, along with everyone else. Except for the giant smear of spidersaurus guts on the floor, nothing appeared out of the ordinary.

"We've got no visual," Cooper said. "Can you re-confirm the location?"

"Um, that's the thing, Coop. It's sort of…moving."

"What are you talking about?" Cooper said. "These things don't move."

"I don't know what to tell you, friend. This one does."

"What's its position?"

"It's about fifty feet down, near the rotunda arch. And I think—yeah, it's definitely heading your way."

They all looked again. But there was still nothing there.

"Simon, we don't see anything!" Grace shouted.

"It's there, dammit! It's coming right at you!"

Cari's heart raced. Her eyes flicked back and forth, searching the storefronts, the faux second-floor windows, anywhere that a Maw might be hiding. She saw nothing. More importantly, she felt nothing. No shaking floor, no cold fingers, no dry throat. Everything was completely normal.

And then everything was gone.

About the Author

S.G. Tasz is a graduate of Lawrence University in Appleton, Wisconsin. Previous writing credits include the web series *Chic*, the award-winning 48-hour Film Project "A Fairly Normal Love Story," and several pieces of short fiction. In addition to plotting the *Dead Mall* gang's next adventure, she is also working on her debut novel, an excerpt for which was the top selection for the 2019 Writer's Bloc Anthology. She lives in Las Vegas with her husband, two cats, and a turtle.

About the Illustrator

Joseph Reedy is an artist based out of Madison, Wisconsin primarily working in the video game and music industries. He also pets lots of doggos.